The Nexus

Operation Gelisko-1

Dibyendu Choudhury

Disclaimer

This book has been published with all reasonable efforts taken to make the material error-free after the consent of the author. No part of this book shall be used, reproduced in any manner whatsoever, without written permission from the author, except in the case of brief quotations embodied in critical articles and reviews. This is a fiction work. Names, characters, places, and incidents either are the product of the author's imagination or are used fictitiously. Any resemblance to actual persons, living or dead, events, or locales is entirely coincidental. It is not intended to offend, disrespect, or criticize any individual's beliefs, religions, or values. Any resemblance to real-life religious figures, events, or practices is purely coincidental and not intended as a deliberate representation or commentary and to be treated as harmless because of the product of imaginative creativity for which even the author is not liable. This work is a fictional creation intended solely for entertainment purposes.

The Author of this book is solely responsible and liable for its content including but not limited to the views, representations, descriptions, statements, information, opinions and references ["Content"]. The Content of this book shall not constitute or be construed or deemed to reflect the opinion or expression of the Publisher or Editor. Neither the Publisher nor Editor endorse or approve the Content of this book or guarantee the reliability, accuracy or completeness of the Content published herein and do not make any representations or warranties of any kind, express or implied, including but not limited to the implied warranties of merchantability, fitness for a particular purpose. The Publisher and Editor shall not be liable whatsoever for any errors, omissions, whether such errors or omissions result from negligence, accident, or any other cause or claims for loss or damages of any kind, including without limitation, indirect or consequential loss or damage arising out of use, inability to use, or about the reliability, accuracy or sufficiency of the information contained in this book.

Dedication

*To the tireless guardians of our nation—
the brave souls who patrol India's borders,
safeguarding her sovereignty with unwavering
dedication.*

*To the martyrs who made the ultimate sacrifice,
laying down their lives for the peace and security of our
homeland—
may their courage inspire generations, and their
memories be eternally honoured.*

*This book stands as a tribute to your selfless service and
enduring legacy.*

Contents

CONTENTS

STATUTORY WARNING

Preface

In a world fuelled by 24/7 news cycles, cryptic headlines, and shadowy reports, it's easy to wonder about the stories behind the stories. Who are the players moving the chess pieces? What drives events that shape the destinies of nations? *The Nexus* was born from this curiosity—a blending of imagination and information that aims to entertain while reflecting on the possibilities lurking in the corners of our reality.

Every thread in this narrative has been drawn from publicly available stories, newspaper headlines, and media reports. While the themes and characters mirror certain real-world issues, it's important to emphasize that this work is purely fictional. The intricate webs of conspiracy, clandestine operations, and geopolitical intrigue are crafted not to provide answers or insights but to thrill, to provoke thought, and perhaps even to amuse.

As you follow Arjun Sinha, the resourceful yet ruthless figure of this tale, and Inspector Shivansh Rathore, the relentless officer determined to expose him, remember that these characters—and the tangled world they navigate—exist in the realm of fiction. The story spans continents

, cultures, and conflicts, from the bustling cities of South Asia to the clandestine corridors of power, but its goal is simple: to engage and entertain.

To my readers, I'm thrilled to share that this book is just the beginning of an exhilarating seven-part series. Due to overwhelming enthusiasm and requests, I am committed to releasing at least three books from this series within the year. The gratitude I feel toward my readers, followers, and critics cannot be overstated; your encouragement fuels every word I write.

Special thanks go to my family for their unconditional love and support, which have been my bedrock throughout this journey. Without them, none of this would have been possible.

Take the journey with an open mind, a good dose of scepticism, and, most importantly, a sense of adventure. Let the fiction play out, the tension keeps you guessing, and the characters come alive in this world of imagination. This is *The Nexus*. Enjoy the ride.

Dibyendu Choudhury

Date: January 2025

Acknowledgments

This book extends its profound gratitude to a multitude of individuals who have contributed significantly to its creation. Foremost among them are my grandparents and parents, who granted me the liberty to delve into the enchanting realm of Indian mythologies and epics. Heartfelt thanks are also due to my wife, daughter, and son, with special recognition to my daughter, who served as the inaugural reader and editor of my earlier books.

Acknowledgments extended to my colleges and school friends, whose encouragement inspired me to craft these stories. However, the primary impetus behind this endeavor stems from my readers, whose consistent encouragement spurred the development of this series and steering it towards a logical conclusion. Given the fictional nature of this book, extensive research and travel were necessary to ensure the authenticity of the content.

This literary endeavor would not have been feasible without the unwavering support, love, and encouragement of my life partner, Debashree. Her uncomplaining nature is deserving of a heartfelt embrace. Special thanks go to our two little imps, Debasmita and Debarko, whose interest in the stories I narrate exceeds their interest in what I write.

Appreciation is owed to my employer and others who maintained their unwavering faith in me, contributing in small but accumulative ways to the eventual publication of this book. As the reader, you are the ultimate judge of my work, holding the right to evaluate it as you see fit.

I would also like to acknowledge the invaluable role played by AI and modern technologies in transforming my paintings and pencil sketches into presentable forms, seamlessly integrated into this book. A special note of thanks is reserved for Microsoft Bing and Image Creator Designer, Canva for their significant contributions to this artistic endeavor.

Gratitude is extended to the readers who always trusted and invested in my book, currently engaged in its perusal. Lastly, a debt of gratitude is owed to the media houses, press and media of India, who have preserved the tradition of storytelling over decades and to our country with its inexhaustible treasure trove of countless stories from where the idea of this series originated.

Dibyendu Choudhury

Prologue: Haldia Port Blast Incident (20 Years Before)

The eerie glow of floodlights illuminated Haldia's docks, creating lengthy shadows on the cargo container stacks. As Shivansh and his group approached their goal, the tension was evident as they moved with experienced stealth. Shivansh was a youthful, daring officer at the time. They believed the intelligence had been reliable. The faint glow of sodium-vapor lamps casts long shadows over the Haldia Port Yard, giving the vast industrial labyrinth of cargo ships, towering cranes, and endless containers a mysterious atmosphere.

The incessant din of machinery drowns out conspiracy whispers, and the air is heavy with the scent of salt, rust, and oil. At the yard's perimeter, abandoned cargo containers from several decades ago stand alone, a quiet tribute to time and neglect. Workers mutter about illegal products and unregistered shipments, speculating on everything from human cargo to smuggled wealth, filling the air with mystery and mistrust.

The harbour is infamous for severe fog coming in from the Bay of Bengal, which provides an ideal cover for illicit transactions. On such occasions, odd people are spotted exchanging briefcases or sealing documents away from the prying eyes of police and other law and enforcement departments. Under the glitter of modernity comes the exploitation of casual dock workers, many of whom vanish after delving too deeply into the yard's operations. Stories about environmental degradation circulate frequently. A black sludge spread around the waterfront, serving as a reminder of oil spills and mismanagement. Fish die in droves, and weird garbage washes up, occasionally horrific enough to make local headlines.

It was believed that Kalu Mastan, Don, the ruler of the port region had brought down Arjun Sinha during this operation. Arjun Sinha was a young boy who was gradually rising to prominence in the dockyard's criminal underworld. This was Shivansh's first field operation for the NCB, and he was still a new recruit. Shivansh was given the responsibility of directing the operation on his own on immediate narcotics dealings by his boss, who saw potential in him to bust the notorious racket by Kalu. Shivansh felt a mix of excitement and nervousness as he prepared to lead his team into uncharted territory.

The setting, the moment, and the element of surprise were all in their favour. Shivansh's heart raced with excitement as they moved in. However, a sudden loud explosion that ripped through the night knocked him off his feet. A flurry of gunshots followed the explosion, and mayhem broke out. The bitter tang of gunpowder blended with the stench of burning rubble. Certain insiders leaked information about his operation, compromising him and his crew, who were then used as bait, facing death. Thankfully, he survived with few in that night but the operation was successful which failed to capture the main culprits except few local dealers.

With his ears ringing from the blast, Shivansh struggled to his feet. The sight in front of him was tumultuous; his crew was engaged in furious combat, bullets were flying everywhere, and there was a strong scent of gunpowder. They were stunned by the crushing counterstrike, which had been meticulously organized as an ambush. Arjun Sinha had fled their clutches amid the smoke and tumult, leaving a trail of loss and ruin in his wake.

Amidst the chaos, Shivansh's gaze fell on a young, injured, and terrified dock worker. The boy's big, terrified, and resolute eyes met his own. Shivansh paused for a second, wondering if the boy was Sinha. Why was he hurt and abandoned if he had planned the explosion?

The urgency of the battle drew Shivansh's focus back to his crew. The image of horror and resolution lingered in his mind, a haunting question mark that would follow him for years, even if the child had been forgotten in the midst of the pandemonium. Whatever the circumstances, Shivansh remembered those huge, scared eyes long after the explosion had receded. As Shivansh urged his workers to continue searching and unloading the container in the quest of the narcotics, he discovered the injured youngster had gone missing. He couldn't shake the impression that there was more to the story than meeting the eyes. Perhaps the youngster is just a pawn in a greater scheme, or maybe he was simply in the wrong place at the wrong time. It served as a reminder of the complexities and uncertainties of the world he lived in, one in which even the most innocent looks may conceal deadly secrets. He nudged the idea that the boy was Sinha. Shivansh speculated that Sinha may have escaped before or during the turmoil.

In reality, the boy who planned the explosion during Shivansh's raid was Sinha. As a result of his injuries sustained in Shivansh's shooting, he pretended to be an innocent, hurt dock worker. He grinned and smirked for the trick until one of his pals, Javed, rescued him. Insanity simmered inside, but his lips twisted into a victorious sneer, and his piercing eyes darted toward the darkness as he saw the officer darting to grab the dealers and the criminals to who Sinha and his associates sold the narcotics a few seconds before.

His eyes burned with the intensity of a raging inferno, reflecting the ferocious resolve of a cornered man. Sinha realized that someone inside leaked and revealed his drug deal to the NCB. It was a chilling realization as the cold grip of betrayal tightened around him, sending shivers down his spine.

The fear gave way to cold, calculating resolve as they heard boots crunching gravel all around them. They were confined. But Sinha's unwavering resolve, fuelled by survival instinct and sheer willpower, kept him from even considering surrender. He grimaced and grabbed the grenade that was fastened to his vest, his mind worked faster. The explosion was his only means of escape, chaos disguised as a plan.

Debris and smoke swirled in all directions as the tremendous detonation shattered the air. Despite the searing pain radiating from his side where shrapnel had torn into him, he pressed on through the chaotic scene, his determination overriding the agony. Distraction, the kind that might buy him the valuable seconds he needed to disappear into the darkness, came at a slight cost in the form of his injuries.

Shivansh's raid continued to find narcotics despite the ongoing gunshots. Sinha saw, in an attempt to regain control, Shivansh gave his squad orders by shout. The local dealers put up a valiant fight back, but the element of surprise was gone. The once-well-planned raid had turned into a last-ditch effort to survive.

After what seemed like a lifetime, reinforcements finally showed up. The piercing screams of sirens mingled with the haunting moans of the injured, filling the air as the echoes of gunshots faded away. With the burden of failure bearing down on him, Shivansh looked around the scene. Although Haldia was meant to be their triumph, it ended up being a nightmare that cost them a lot of innocent manpower.

In order to remove any evidence of their ambush and wash away the operation's sign, he gave his squad the order to fire the dockside forklift after the seizure of narcotics and a few hoodlums.

Shivansh's career began with a bloody and smoky prologue that served as a sobering reminder of the terrible reality of combating organized crime. Loss was a part of the beginning, but so was the determination to never be outplayed again. Shivansh was aware that this was only the beginning of his protracted and difficult journey.

The boy's expression served as a clear reminder of collateral damages in such operations where innocent lives are sacrificed. His career began with a bloody and smoky prologue, serving as a sobering reminder of the terrible reality of combating organized crime. This was only the beginning of a protracted and difficult journey ahead for Shivansh.

The globe saw the news the following day.

Chapter-1
Kamarajar Port Operation

Chapter 1: Kamarajar Port Operation (Today)

The rain today battered the corrugated steel roofs of the warehouses along Kamarajar Port, formerly Chennai Port. Each drip appeared to echo the weight of the task at hand. A key hub of India's marine commerce, the port was now the centre of a dark conspiracy that extended well beyond its steel-grey seas. A group of NCB agents and local cops huddled together in a darkened alley beside Warehouse 17, their expressions grim with purpose, while the storm raged over the entire city. They were aware that they needed to move quickly to solve the enigma and nab the kingpin beside recovery of the narcotics within the port's fortifications. They were the only ones who could avert the looming catastrophe.

The eyes of Indian Narcotics Bureau (NCB) Inspector Shivansh Rathore darted across the docks as he stood beneath a warehouse awning. The restless sea, where cargo ships loomed like dark spectres, was illuminated by the pale glimmer of sodium lights. His trench coat did nothing to shelter him from drizzle, but it wasn't the cold that made him tremble. The sensation that he was being watched persisted when he was waiting there. He was aware that failure was not an option and that the stakes were huge. He inhaled deeply as he prepared for the perilous task ahead, resolved to cut the web of corruption that threatened India. He bore the responsibility for the country's destiny being a responsible officer.

They raided an office a few hours ago, which led them to believe that something suspicious was going to occur here tonight. The "MV Scorpion" might have a drug curtail which was docked at the port. Even if it was founded on a few gut instincts, it might not only be the beginning. The ramifications were sometimes more important than the consignment's astounding worth. These might be linked to corruption, arms smuggling, and human trafficking.

The lighter briefly illuminated Sinha's chiselled face as he lit a cigarette to calm himself in warehouse 12.

Riya identified him and murmured "There he is."

He must grasp the kingpin. Sometimes, prevention is better than cure. It is possible to hold the person in charge of the Andaman-Chennai corridor accountable for overseeing a money-laundering, people trafficking, and smuggling of narcotics red handed. He was driven, and it was a risky game based on gut instincts. After storming an office of that man with his aide Riya and his squad, he arrived directly from Santhome Road in the Mylapore with the intention of apprehending him with his likely smuggled shipment.

Unaware of the impending storm, the dockworkers carried on with their duties, securing goods and moving containers. There was a lot of tension in the air as shadows flowed in and out of the alleys between the warehouses. Every face seemed like a potential enemy and criminal, every rustle of movement like a threat. He couldn't get rid of the impression that danger was present everywhere he looked at the busy bustle going on around him. He was aware that one mistake could cost him everything, and the stakes were higher than ever. He was getting closer to capture the enemy and bust its shadowy underbelly with each step.

The conversation and exchange with Delhi with Kavita Nair Madam, as well as the coded texts from her team received, suggested something much more dangerous than a drug gang. But more crucial at that point to hold the breath, adjusting with the increasing pressure from superiors to shut down the shadowy enterprise and capture the kingpin before it causes mayhem. Up until now, Riya was not aware of that piece of information.

A group of men gathered in tight conversation, their silhouettes sharp against the floodlights saturated with rain. A man who could only be Arjun Sinha stood in the middle, his gestures demanding attention and his posture displaying power.

Shivansh was pulled back to the present by Riya's voice and a crackling on his earpiece.

"There he is," Riya muttered.

The faint rumble of a truck engine came before Shivansh could answer. Riya requested reinforcements consisting of local police and customs officials for this seizure when a blacked-out car pulled into view, its doors opening to show guys with heavy weapons. The anxiety increased as the atmosphere changed.

Shivansh keyed the mic. "Alpha Team, be ready. On my signal, we proceed.

But just as they were about to attack, the port was filled with a deafening metallic clang. One of the dockworkers had unintentionally overturned a crate. Every eye was drawn to their hiding place as the disturbance broke the delicate calm.

Silently acknowledging Riya, they prepared themselves for the future and were prepared to take on any obstacles that could arise.

 They discovered a viewpoint that provided a clear view of The Scorpion close to Warehouse 17. With its lights barely penetrating the darkness, the ship was a huge silhouette against the turbulent sea. On the deck, men were moving like shadows, clearing their goods to the port and getting ready for the illegal trade.

Shivansh commanded, "Proceed," his voice firm in spite of the excitement pumping through his body. He moved quickly, the wet ground muffling his footsteps. He gave the order for his crew to spread out, protecting every exit, as he got closer to Warehouse 17. The faint light inside the warehouse showed a sight of well-planned anarchy. Inconspicuous labelled crates were being put into trucks that were not tagged. With hoods and shadows covering their faces, men dressed in black attire moved with a sense of efficiency.

As he huddled behind a pile of rusting oil drums, Shivansh's heart raced, and his nostrils were filled with the pungent odour of wet metal and grease. Smugglers were packing containers with fictitious shipping labels in the warehouse in front of him, which was a hive of illegal activity. Amidst the quiet hum of machinery, the enormous area was filled with the bustle of hurried voices in numerous languages. This was the focal point of a multi-continental operation, so it wasn't just another bust.

The tactical unit dispersed like shadows as he made a small hand gesture to his crew. It was a tense time, full of anxiety. Shivansh was sweating profusely, but his concentration remained unwavering.

Bang!

Someone fired a shot from which side not understood but no time to wait, so Shivansh gave the command right away.

He muttered, "Go," into his communications.

The quite broke like glass. His group charged on, yelling orders as mayhem broke out. In response, the smugglers pulled out their firearms and dispersed like light-caught rats. Splintering sounds of crates being smashed apart blended with the crackling of gunfire that reverberated off the steel walls.

Shivansh ran with the precision of a tightrope walker, each step calculated to navigate the chaos around him. Avoiding flying debris, he fired swift, suppressive bullets that instantly rendered enemies' unconscious.

Bang!

Bang!

He got closer to the centre of the operation with each takedown. He searched the confusion for something or someone that caught his attention.

Then he caught sight of him.

A man exuding authority stood in the centre of the warehouse, giving the other smugglers directives. He was tall, his chiselled face half hidden by a waterproof cap brim, his keen eyes scanning the surroundings. He wasn't just any operator; his actions were assured and purposeful. The person tugging the strings was this one.

A surge of intuition gripped Shivansh as he whispered to himself, "That's him."

He sprinted after saying, "Target sighted," into his communications. "Avoid letting him get away."

With the tiniest glimmer of recognition in his eyes, the man halted for a moment upon seeing Shivansh. Then, like a predator, he turned and ran farther into the maze of machinery and crates.

Shivansh pursued. As he weaved through the tight tunnels, the air was heavy with dust and excitement. As he guided Shivansh through a maze intended to confuse him, the man moved quickly and deliberately. Shivansh remained close, his concentration unwavering, his breathing steady.

Shivansh briefly saw the man's silhouette disappearing into the darkness of a huge storage facility as they turned a corner. The gloomy atmosphere that the tall cargo stacks and dim lighting created amplified every groan and echo.

"You're in a tight spot!" Shivansh yelled in a forceful voice. "There is nowhere else to flee to."

(Quiet.)

Shivansh moved slowly forward, his weapon out. His keen eyes looked around, all his senses alert. He turned just in time to see the man lunging for him from behind a stack of crates after hearing a tiny scuffling sound to the left.

With Shivansh's weapon skittering across the floor, the impact drove them both sprawling. Shivansh was a well-trained and skilled fighter as well, but the man was powerful and had vicious, effective motions too. He deflected a blow to his face and retaliated with a quick stab to the ribs that caused a groan of agony.

The fight was intense, with each blow being well-planned and lethal. They struggled in the gloom, gasping for air, until Shivansh finally struck hard enough to knock the man down. Pulling a hidden dagger from his boot to press on the man's throat, Shivansh used a sudden surge of strength to pin him down.

Shivansh declared in a chilling whisper, "It's over, Sinha."

Unwavering in his defiance, the man grinned.

"Do you believe this makes a difference? You're competing in a much larger arena with a lot smaller game."

Shivansh's hold became firmer. "We'll check that out later."

Shortly after, his squad showed in, secured the man in restraints, and assessed the situation. Subdued smugglers, broken crates that contained no drugs, illicit weaponry, and counterfeit money were not found too. Absolutely nothing! It was spotless. But as expected, everything ought to have been present.

Shivansh stood over the captured man, his mind racing as the excitement faded. He was aware that he had lost the game, so this was no win. He tried to figure wrong. First, why were they shooting at them if everything was clean? Then, why were these folks acting and playing like smugglers?

"Clean the entire facility and bag the evidence." He gave his crew the instruction, "We cannot leave this place without any evidence." "We're arresting him. I want Riya to be on his interrogation, so call her. Raid the ship as well.

Shivansh looked around the warehouse as they escorted the man away, the scope of the operation beginning to dawn on him. This went beyond smuggling and drugs. He lacked evidence, but this was more about power, corruption, and the evil powers that profited from mayhem. He was completely unaware that the true storm was just getting started when the storm outside started to lessen, though.

The air was thick with the acrid stench of gunpowder as the team led the captured leader out of the warehouse. Shivansh walked with his weapon lowered but ready, his senses still sharp. The operation had been a success; he didn't get any evidence so far at the warehouse, but he knew better than to let his guard down entirely. Still, some hope is left from the ship.

As they stepped into the open, the night was eerily quiet except for the distant hum of the city. The moonlight reflected off the wet pavement, casting a silver sheen over the scene. Shivansh turned to Riya, who was guiding another officer through securing evidence from the ship. He was about to speak when a blinding flash illuminated the sky.

Boom!

The explosion hit like a thunderclap.

The ground shook violently, throwing Shivansh off his feet and sending a shockwave through the area. The deafening roar of the blast drowned out all other sounds. Flames erupted from a parked van nearby and shards of debris rained down like deadly confetti. The warehouse windows shattered, sending glass flying in every direction.

Shivansh groaned as he pushed himself up, his ears ringing and his vision blurred. He blinked against the stinging smoke, his heart sinking as he surveyed the scene. Officers lay scattered on the ground, some motionless, others writhing in pain. The acrid smoke mixed with the metallic scent of blood.

"Riya!" he shouted; his voice sounded hoarse. His eyes searched frantically until he saw her sprawled on the ground, blood trickling from a gash on her temple. Her breathing was shallow, her face pale.

Riya scrambled to his side, his hands trembling as he checked her pulse. It was faint but steady. He experienced some brief relief, but it quickly vanished in favour of a chilling dread. The explosion had been no accident, it was planted in car bomb.

"Sir!" a wounded officer coughed, pointing toward the smouldering remains of the transport vehicle. Shivansh's stomach dropped as he realized the car bomb was planted and the handcuffed leader would be nowhere to be seen.

"Was it a plot to kill the kingpin, or was the bomb planted to kill them? Why all of these? No evidence of smuggling, still why?" Shivansh's mind overwhelmed with questions.

Through the haze, he spotted shadows moving quickly away from the chaos. A black SUV screeched to a halt just beyond the perimeter, its doors swinging open. Several figures emerged from the smoke, dragging their people and leaving the kingpin injured alone on the road to get him arrested.

"No!" Shivansh roared, surging to his feet despite the pain lancing through his body. He stumbled after them, the sharp pain of his bleeding legs fuelling his determination. Gunfire erupted again, forcing him to dive for cover as the vehicle sped off, its taillights disappearing into the darkness. Blood was seeping from his body; blood was everywhere.

"Damn it!" Shivansh slammed his fist into the ground, the frustration and fury boiling inside him. His hands were scraped and bleeding, but the pain felt inconsequential compared to the bitter taste of the failure.

The scene around him was a nightmare. Officers were shouting, calling for medics and trying to regain control amidst the chaos. Shivansh turned back to Riya, his heart sinking further as he saw the severity of her injuries. He gently cradled her head, his voice soft but urgent.

"Riya, stay with me," he pleaded. Her eyelids fluttered and she managed a weak nod.

Medics arrived moments later, working frantically to stabilize the injured. Shivansh reluctantly let them take Riya, his gaze lingering on her as they loaded her onto a stretcher to the ambulance to shift the injured to the hospital for medications. He looked like he lost a very close relative.

The bitter truth weighed heavily on him—the operation had been compromised and sabotaged from within. However, the explosion had been meticulously planned, timed to create maximum disruption and tried to kill the kingpin too. Someone in their network had betrayed them, feeding information to their enemies.

"Then why did they leave the kingpin alive for the trial? Was it a double sabotage from both the sides?"

As Shivansh stood amidst the devastation, a storm of emotions raged within him—guilt, anger and an unyielding resolve. He clenched his fists, his jaw tightening.

"They've deceived us and now declared war," he muttered under his breath. *"And I'm not letting them win. We nabbed your kingpin. We will use him."*

With his team regrouping and reinforcements arriving, Shivansh knew the battle had just initiated. The kingpin was nabbed to get further information. Shivansh vowed he wouldn't stop and would slowly reach the bottom of this case. Something was wrong there.

Reinforcements swarmed the docks, quickly overpowering the remaining assailants. Within minutes, the area was made secured.

After few hours the daylight came in, Shivansh and Riya exchanged their glance in the hospital, a silent acknowledgment of their joint operation and joint failure. Both received the medications and their wounds were cleaned and bandaged.

"We couldn't make it, sir. Sorry, I just failed you because I trusted my gut feelings and thought that something would have been revealed here. But…" Riya murmured; nothing came out from her mouth. She was looking desperate, dejected and injured too.

Shivansh nodded, his adrenaline slowly ebbing. "This is just the beginning, Riya; we've nabbed the several people along with the kingpin. Let's get some info out of him." He said, echoing the sentiment that had driven them from the start. "But it's a good lesson and start for you; even I got my beginning the same way at NCB in Haldia long back."

The storm finally began to abate, the rain easing to a steady drizzle in the morning sky of Chennai.

As they surveyed the scene next later, they realized the entire scene was made clean much before their arrival. Shivansh acknowledged the daunting distance still to cover in the ongoing battle against the criminal empire; they were just scratching the surface. But last night, they had taken a crucial step and nabbed one of their adversaries' important heads, and that was a victory worth savouring, which might lead them to find the trail.

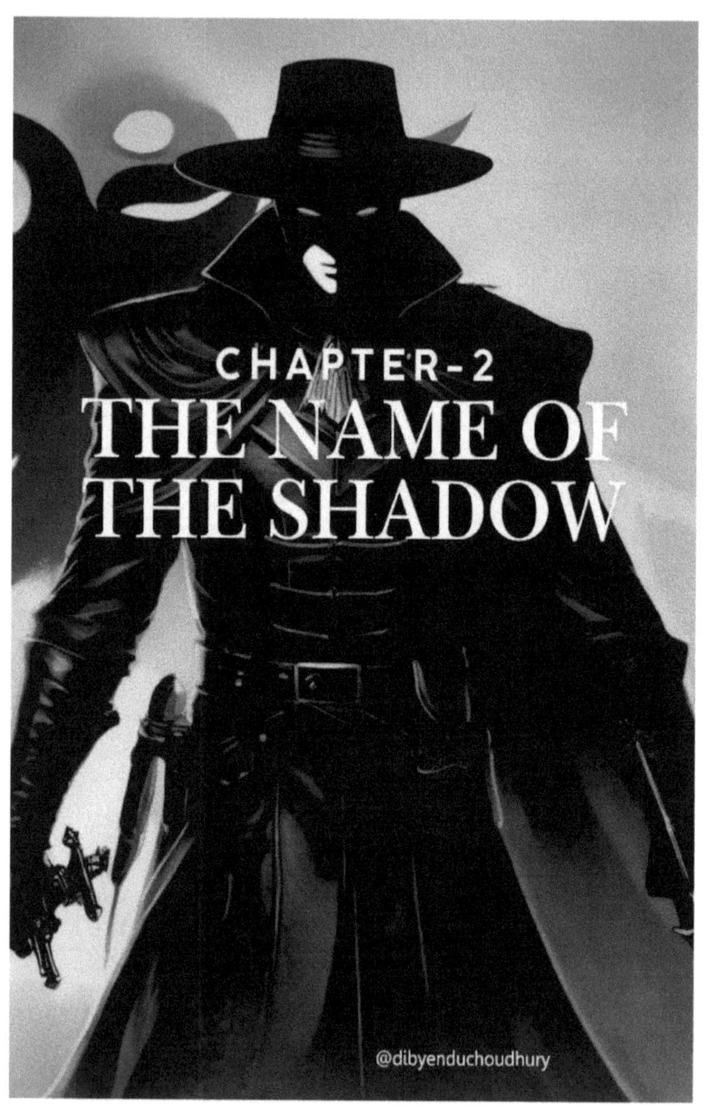

CHAPTER-2
THE NAME OF THE SHADOW
@dibyenduchoudhury

Chapter 2: The Name of the Shadow. (Few Hours before)

In his pocket, Shivansh's phone buzzed. It was Shivansh's assistant, Riya Menon, an NCB analyst who had a talent for finding the most elusive leads. Despite the rain's static, her voice was clear and urgent.

"We've got a lead, sir!" Riya's words relieved the tension in the room.

"Can we meet in next 30 minutes at the former warehouse on San Thome Highroad in Mylapore? I believe we're at last on to something significant."

Eager to find out what new mystery Riya had discovered, he quickly gathered his essentials, slipping into his raincoat before venturing out.

 Without introducing herself, she stated, "We have intelligence. Sir."

She continued as Shivansh started his vehicle and Riya was on speaker "The name Arjun Sinha just came up. A logistics tycoon based out of Andaman, today Sinha is in Chennai. Although he lives in the Andaman and other cities majorly international in Asia pacific region. According to intelligence, he is in this city on the ground for this crucial operation today, it seems. Although he appears to be innocent on paper, he may be the mastermind behind the Andaman-Chennai heroin and smuggling trade, according to unofficial sources."

His thoughts were racing with the potential outcomes and ramifications of this lead as Riya shared the fresh information about "Arjun Sinha" and this name never disclosed so far. He couldn't quite identify the name, but it seemed familiar.

A sombre veil draped over the city as the rain cascaded down in relentless torrents. In the distance, thunder roared, a warning sound reverberated across the streets signed the prolonged night of thunderstorm with rain on the city, forecasted in a FM radio channel of the car.

The mood was equally tensed inside the darkened office. Long shadows were created on the walls by the overhead bulb's dim glow, reflecting the storm that was building both inside and outside of their business. The gentle drumming of raindrops on the glass mingled with the faint scent of wet earth, enveloping Shivansh Rathore's mind as he stood by the window, lost in contemplation. He crushed his cigarette with the sole of his boot after flicking it to the ground. His face was a mixture of concentration and annoyance. The scent of stale coffee, moist paper, and the subtle hint of anxiousness filled the room.

Riya laid out a number of documents over the table, including satellite photos, cargo vessel photos, and shipping logs. As she spoke, her keen eyes raced between the pages.

"What do we possess about him?" Shivansh's voice broke the oppressive silence.

"He owns a fleet of cargo ships, all registered under shell companies in Singapore, Sri Lanka, and Dubai, we traced it all." Riya said without raising her gaze.

"Since he has officials working for him, customs inspections have never raised a single red flag on his shipments. The "M.V. Scorpion", one of his ships, is reportedly docking at Kamarajar Port tonight, according to our intelligence."

Shivansh furrowed his brow. "What is the history of the Scorpion?"

A page was tapped by Riya's finger. "It has stopped at Chennai Port six times in the past two weeks, each time arriving from the Andaman. Although it is officially registered for routine repair at Andaman, there is a strange amount of information in the marine records. The transit logs for this week are not available at all."

"Not available, what do you mean? Maybe it is not updated yet." Shivansh's voice became piercing.

Riya gave a nod. "Either the records have been altered, or the Scorpion's movements being purposefully hidden. I checked port authorities and all other records. The worst part is that our intelligence indicates the cargo for tonight may be extremely precious and hazardous. We believe that

"Cocaine" or other illegal substances are being smuggled through this ship tonight."

As Shivansh took in the information, his jaw tensed. "The Scorpion is hence the foundation of this suspicion, you mean? We may miss our finest opportunity to reveal the entire scam if we let this shipment pass. Have you shared Customs the information?"

Leaning forward, Riya fixed her gaze on him. "Not yet Sir; if we catch it tonight, we'll cut off their supply chain and show that their operations aren't as inviolable as they believe. I feel they have people inside customs."

Shivansh turned to face the throng forming in the space, the desk lamp's shaky light illuminated their faces.

"This is not an accident. They have something planned." Riya paused.

As he started giving directions, the room hummed with a subdued eagerness.

"Secure the docks and coordinate with the coast guard, local police. We must secure the area and make sure that nobody enters or exits without permission. To blend in with port employees, assign plainclothes officers. Get the Scorpion's schematics,

Riya. Before we arrive, I want to know every inch of that ship. And be prepared with a backup plan because this could go wrong at any time."

The group proceeded deliberately, assembling equipment and completing their plan.

Shivansh turned to Riya while he checked his weapon and grabbed his jacket.

"This is it. Tonight, might be the breakthrough we've been waiting for, if we're correct. However, if we're mistaken..."

"We're not incorrect, I have a strong gutt feelings, Sir." Riya interrupted, her eyes revealed the assertive feelings behind them he found her firm voice with strong belief.

Shivansh nodded briefly. "Then, let's ensure that we are prepared for anything within few hours."

With measured words, she seated beside him and began, while Shivansh embarked for the port in his SUV, "Arjun Sinha is a ghost. No less-than-perfect, he has no digital footprint. His official documents are immaculate—too much clear and clean, really. However, I've made some connections. A meeting is being discussed for tonight. Big players, high stakes. All of this is taking place in the port tonight."

Shivansh's knuckles tightened his grasp on the wheel. "The port," he said again, his thoughts rushing through the many meanings. "Who's attending?"

Riya took a quick look at the dimly lit iPad on her lap. "Sources identify important cartel members. This isn't a typical smuggling operation. They may consolidate, but they are here to bargain. And it's the ideal cover now that the M V Scorpion has arrived. There, we have chance to catch them and chop off the snake's head."

Shivansh found himself relying on her unflinching confidence. This wasn't just a flop idea; they were entering perilous terrain. It was worth risking the greatest possible stakes—a direct confrontation with the cartel's leadership.

"Are you certain about this information?" In an urgent tone, Shivansh reaffirmed with Riya.

"As certain as we can get," Riya said, looking into his eyes. "This is our chance. They will solidify their position if we allow this gathering to go without opposition. However, if we attack right away, we destroy the basis for their activities."

"But if we fail, they get the alert too." she added.

With her words weighing heavily on his shoulders, Shivansh nodded. He had faith in her intuition and resolve. He made too many sacrifices and gone too far to let this chance pass. He used to be just as vivacious as Riya, but he eventually realized that occasionally being overly anxious and adventurous ruined the whole game.

The proposal was bold, bordering on reckless, but there was no space for doubt. "We're moving in," Shivansh declared resolutely, his determination becoming stronger by the second.

As they neared the harbour, the rain grew heavier and the storm grew larger as though the sky itself could sense the impending collision. With cranes towering over the landscape like silent giants and cargo containers stacked like monolithic walls, the expansive docks were bustling with activity.

After killing the engine, Shivansh parked the SUV in a discrete location close to the perimeter. The crew, cloaked in black, seamlessly melded into the shadows, their movements calculated and soundless, adding an air of ominous anticipation to the unfolding events.

He looked and told to Riya. "This is it. There is no space for error. We remain sharp while you stay close to me."

Riya had a determined yet tense look on her face. "Sir, I will not overlook this. Let us complete it."

Nodding, they stepped out of the car, their weapons and clothes instantly soaked in the rain. In a synchronized effort with the squad, Shivansh fine-tuned his waterproof cap, his hushed commands cutting through the ambient noise of the port. "We all need to take the position. Keeping an eye on the target."

The reverberation of industrial gear concealed their approach as they moved through the tangle of shipping containers. Shivansh was acutely aware of everything, examining every sound and shadow.

Riya pointed to a clearing in the distance where the glow of portable lights and the sound of soft voices suggested activities. They squatted behind a pile of crates and watched.

The rain had increased by the time they arrived in the evening at Kamarajar Port, dark sky transformed the dockyards into a labyrinth of slippery surfaces and hazy shadows. The air hummed with the ceaseless activity of freight operations even in such hush weather.

Shivansh's senses prickled with anticipation as his sharp gaze swept over the surroundings. There was a strange feeling. Eyes darting toward the Scorpion, moored like a sleeping beast at the far end of the port, dockworkers were moving with a casual face that seemed almost practiced.

Shivansh saw people transporting containers from the ship to trucks that were waiting through the raindrops.

A gnawing unease coiled in the depths of Shivansh's stomach, refusing to dissipate as they prepared to move forward, a blend of apprehension and steely determination in his gaze. He was prepared to take on whatever lay ahead of them in Kamarajar, even though he knew it would not be simple. Shivansh led the route into the night with his squad by his side, intent on learning the truth about the enigmatic circumstances that had led them to this perilous location. Despite the huge stakes, Shivansh was determined to see it through to the conclusion, regardless of the challenges they would encounter.

CHAPTER-3
Pent House Command

Chapter 3: The Penthouse Command (24 Hrs Before)

The penthouse towered over Chennai's sprawling skyline, perched like an emperor surveying its domain. It is located in the rapidly transforming neighbourhood of Perambur along Mahabalipuram Road; it stood as a beacon of opulence amidst the evolving urban landscape. Due to the Chennai Municipal Authorities' (CMA) relaxation of the Floor Space Index (FSI) rules, high-rise developments were now sprouting up everywhere like weeds. Lots of booming office-space leasing and the catalytic effect of the burgeoning Metro rail network. Yet, amidst this architectural revolution, the penthouse exuded an eerie calm, detached from the chaos it overlooked.

Inside, heavy velvet drapes hung like sentinels, muting the city's noise to a distant hum. The soft strains of jazz filtered through hidden speakers, adding an unsettling tranquillity to the lavishly furnished space. Crystal decanters of whiskey and wine glimmered on a sideboard and a leather couch luxuriously faced the floor-to-ceiling windows.

Arjun Sinha, the elusive kingpin, sat in his sanctuary, his piercing eyes scanning the cityscape as if it were a chessboard. His empire spanned across continents, his power cemented in deals inked in shadows and whispered in alleys. This evening, however, his calm veneer was tinged with unease.

Behind him, a digital dashboard projected shipping manifests with encrypted communications and live feeds from key locations across the world of his shipping fleets and cargos. Tonight, "The Scorpion" will be docked at Kerala; we changed the course and route. His men were in position, yet something gnawed at his gut.

Due to the Bureau's activity, they had to do this—it was not too much for comfort.

His lieutenant, Javed, entered the room with his usual briskness, breaking the silence.

"The shipment is secured and rerouted, boss. Another vessel we named "The Scorpion" in Kamarajar for their seizure. We've got eyes on us. Shivansh and his team are moving. We intercepted their chatter—they're planning to hit the port anytime tonight. Already they are at our Mylapore office and eventually they will seal it and grab some of our documents."

Arjun's lips curled into a wry smile. "Shivansh Rathore," he mused. "The man just doesn't quit. So far, they never have anything against me."

Javed shifted uncomfortably. "He's persistent unless we stop him. This isn't the usual lot of bumbling officers."

Arjun leaned back, swirling the whiskey in his glass. "Persistent, yes. But persistence isn't enough. They're playing checkers, Javed. We're playing chess. I like such an opponent; it sharpens my brain too."

Javed hesitated before speaking again. "Do you want me to deploy the contingency team? We can buy some time—create enough chaos to throw them off."

Arjun waved him off. "Not yet." Allow them to come and perform the necessary at the end. Allow them to believe they are making progress, and it will happen. It makes the final blow much sweeter. Checkmate! Only ensure that none of our critical contacts attend tonight's meeting. Allow Shivansh and his troops to capture or kill our adversaries."

Javed nodded and left the room, leaving Arjun alone with his thoughts. The city stretched before him, glittering with lights that masked its underbelly of corruption, crime and desperation. He thrived in that underbelly, feeding off its chaos and weaving it into his meticulously crafted empire for so long.

It was a rainy day forecasted with a thunderstorm ahead. As the rain was falling relentlessly, pattering against the glass, Arjun's phone buzzed. He answered it without hesitation, his tone clipped and direct. "What is it?"

The voice on the other end spoke rapidly, delivering news that made Arjun smile. He leaned forward, his fingers tightening around the glass. "You're sure?" he asked, his voice icy.

The confirmation came and Arjun hung up, his mind racing. Shivansh was closer than he'd anticipated. It was time to recalibrate, to stay two steps ahead as always. His bait will work out.

He moved slowly through the room to the posh balcony. Below, the city thrived in its noisy, messy glory. To most, it was a city of dreams, of opportunity. To him, it was a labyrinth—a playground where he could move unseen, manipulate the game and crush anyone who dared challenge him to date.

He knew, however, that the stakes would soon be higher than ever. The Bureau's movements, the illicit shipment and the web of friendships he had created over the years were all merging in an unstoppable storm. While Arjun thrived in storms, he could also feel the shifting winds.

Arjun Sinha sat in the centre of it all, a man in complete command of his world. The leather couch he lounged on was custom-made, its deep mahogany hue matching the polished wood of the coffee table in front of him. On it lay the tools of his trade: shipping manifests, coded messages and maritime maps of the Andaman Sea. These weren't just documents; they were blueprints for an empire—an empire built on deceit, fear, the shimmering promise of illicit wealth and blood.

Arjun swirled his whiskey, the amber liquid catching the dim light and took a slow sip. The burst at Haldia, which had sent shockwaves through his network, was nothing more than a deception. He was used to setting up decoys; they were the cost of doing business.

As he gazed out over the city, Arjun's mind was already strategizing. He knew the next moves he needed to make to keep his operation running smoothly. The penthouse was his command centre in India, a place where he could think clearly and plan without interruption to rule the world. The muted sounds of the city below were a constant reminder of the world he controlled from his lofty perch.

The door to the penthouse opened and a shadowy figure stepped in. It was Rajesh, one of Arjun's most trusted lieutenants. He moved with a blend of urgency and deference, knowing that while Arjun valued his insights, the stakes were high and mistakes were not tolerated.

"Sir," Rajesh began, his voice steady, "the latest shipment has been rerouted. It should reach its destination without further issues. We managed the port authorities."

Arjun nodded, his gaze never leaving the cityscape. "And the others?"

"They will be distracted and deceived. They're focused on getting some clue, trying to connect the dots. They won't see this coming."

A slow smile spread across Arjun's face. "Good. Ensure all loose ends are tied up. We can't afford another interruption."

Rajesh hesitated, then spoke again. "There's one more thing. Our informants in the Bureau have indicated that Inspector Rathore and his team are becoming a bigger problem. They're tenacious."

Arjun's smile faded. "I am aware of Shivansh Rathore... He's resourceful. But he's also just a man with limited resources, Rajesh. Find out everything about him. Weaknesses, routines, family—everything. I want to know what makes him tick. Now, you go to the port instead of me and ensure everything is alright and buy time."

Rajesh nodded and left the room, leaving Arjun alone with his thoughts. As the night deepened, the jazz from the speakers seemed to blend with the city's hum, creating a haunting symphony. Arjun refilled his glass with whiskey.

He knew he was playing a dangerous game, but it was one he was groomed with. The thrill of outmanoeuvring his enemies, staying one step ahead, was what drove him always through deceptions. And he had no intention of stopping now when everything was happening as he wished.

Chapter-4
THE GAME OF
DECEPTION

Chapter 4: The Game of Deception

It was a gentle but purposeful knock on the door again. Arjun gave it a quick glance and a single nod. Javed entered the room again. Javed was wiry and always on the edge, moving with the anxious intensity of someone who trusted and knew too much.

"The shipment to Kerala has reached," Javed stated calmly and quietly.

"However, there is a lot of conversation going on here. The Bureau is conducting an investigation in Chennai Port."

Arjun smiled wider. "Let them sniff around; dogs will only find trouble." We'll be two steps ahead when they realize what's going on."

As he leaned forward, his eyes sparkled with a combination of cold calculation and arrogance.

"Direct the captains to carry out their planned actions. Any deviation will be met with suspicion. We spent too much work on building this corridor to be concerned.

Javed hesitated. "The discussion is not only about the region. RAW also entered into it. They have been working with the Coast Guard to intercept ships near the Andaman routes too."

Arjun's face clouded as the room seemed to grow colder.

 "Really? Interesting. Finally, our friends in Delhi seem to be waking up. I had been waiting for them." He deliberately thumped his glass down.

Javed spoke nervously. "We have to be careful, Boos. Their involvement could make things more challenging. They are renowned for their effectiveness."

Arjun was taller than Javed and ruled the room. "They cannot stop us, whether they like it or not. Today or tomorrow, they would have also engaged, even if we like it or not. However, we always remain more adaptive and flexible than them, Javed. That is how we have survived. Tonight, we leave mainland India for Sri Lanka so that the other consignment coming from Myanmar can reach Chittagong Port, Bangladesh. Make the necessary arrangements." His voice was filled with frigid resolve and a harsh growl.

He again walked to the glassed balcony, looking out at the skyline. The lights of Chennai, a bustling metropolis unaware of the evil plans going on beneath its shadow, glistened in the distance. Arjun's thoughts were racing, ruthlessly assessing what he should do next.

Arjun said, facing away from Javed, "Tell our contacts to keep watchful. Double the security for the incoming shipments here. And find out who is leaking information to the Bureau. I want them settled discretely and promptly."

Javed took notes frantically and nodded. "I will see to that."

Javed started to leave when Arjun said, "One more thing. We have to send out a message to distract them. Something that will divert RAW and the Bureau and make them temporarily switch to lighter mode."

In a low voice, Sinha said something to Javed.

Javed paused, realizing the significance of his statements. "I understand, sir. I will take care of it."

After Javed left, Arjun went to his desk in the middle of the room, already planning for the future. He understood that this was a critical time. Now the stakes were higher, and any slip-up could undo everything he had worked so hard for. But Arjun Sinha flourished under pressure. It was in these tough circumstances that his genuine brilliance emerged.

He poured another glass of amber whiskey, which swirled in the dim light. As he sipped, his thoughts turned to the convoluted web of promises and deceptions that had led him to this point. Because confidence was a limited resource in his environment, he used it as a two-edged sword.

Arjun pulled a secure phone from his drawer and dialled a number. He said, "Plan B is in order," without warning. "Start using our sleeper cells. I want a thorough examination of the port and surrounding area at Chittagong. If someone gets too close, make it look like there is a public disturbance."

The speaker on the other end acknowledged the order and then cut off. Arjun leaned back on his chair with a sour sense of accomplishment. As the night deepened, Arjun sat in his palace of riches and power, strategizing his next move with the cold precision of an experienced strategist.

Arjun's mind was racing with possibilities and ideas, each more devious than the last. So yet, no one has managed to outmanoeuvre him. Not by RAW, the Bureau, or Shivansh Rathore. Arjun was ready to take on any task, no matter how risky the journey.

He took a final, resolute swallow of his whiskey and returned his focus to the task at hand. For years, the penthouse had served as his escape, allowing him to plan his next move. The metropolis below was a real, breathing organism, yet he dominated from above. Every movement he made created ripples and tonight, as he planned his next move, those ripples quickly turned into waves. Arjun took one final look at the materials and maps spread out in front of him before beginning to pack. The Andaman water, the intricate network of water channels, and the coded communications all told a story of immense wealth, corruption, and power. He knew Inspector Rathore would not surrender until he was defeated. But Arjun was prepared. He was eager to start playing the game, which had just begun. As the lights of Chennai faded under him, he recognized that the main battle lied ahead, and he needed to face it full on.

After carefully lighting a few incense sticks on his room's table, he proceeded to the kitchen to slowly open the gas oven so that it was flowing slowly throughout the entire space. The LPG would eventually discover the fire like a ticking time bomb.

He glanced at his command centre once more for the last time before locking the door and heading for the elevator. A black SUV stood still in the portico, Javed behind the wheel, calmly waiting. The truck slowly made its way up the Mahabalipuram route to a small fishing village; in a few hours, the sun would rise over the sea. A boat was waiting to transport them from the Indian shore to his ship in Sri Lanka.

During the silent journey, the only sounds were the constant hum of the motor and the far-off roll of the waves. Even though Arjun felt the weight of the night's task pressing down on him, he strengthened himself with the willpower that had seen him through countless trials before. The true test of his cunning and will was about to begin.

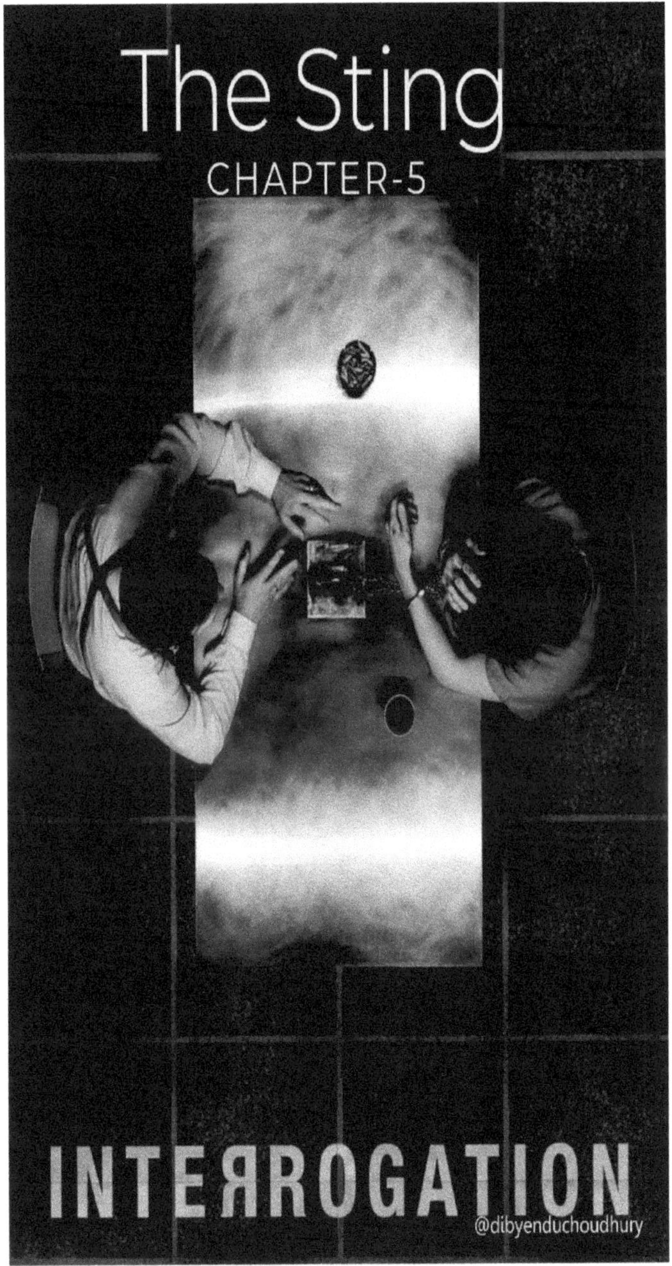
The Sting
CHAPTER-5
INTERROGATION
@dibyenduchoudhury

Chapter 5: The Sting (Next Day after Kamarajar Port Operation)

Shivansh, severely bruised and bandaged, wrapped his leg and body. He leaned against the hospital bed frame, his face etched with tiredness and frustration. The sterile fragrance of antiseptic permeated the air, mixed with the faint metallic flavour of blood that lingered in his memories of the previous night's slaughter. Riya sat across from him in a chair in the distance, her arm immobilized in a sling, her face pallid but her eyes brimming with the same rage he felt.

"Do you still remember?" Shivansh inquired, his tone low and gravelly, "Before I could even signal the move?" A solitary gunshot broke the silence. Workers spread like ants before arriving—armed to the teeth, rifles in hand. "Who fired?

Riya nodded grimly, her gaze remote as she relived the mayhem in her mind.

"Sir, it's a set-up. A damn trap. They have us surrounded, and worse—there's nothing. No drugs, no smuggled goods. That warehouse and 'The Scorpion' are spotless, just like their office." She winced, shifting her injured arm against the cold armrest of the hospital chair.

"I can't even believe this, with all the intel and hours of planning, we walk right into their game exactly the way they wanted and end up empty-handed. This morning, one of their hideouts is found completely burned down in the OMR."

Shivansh clinched his hands. The night's events whirled in his mind: the explosion outside the warehouse, his coworkers' screams, and the thick smoke that filled the air as chaos broke out. They had lost fine guys, bold officers who believed in the mission. The reality of it twisted his stomach.

"It was a deception, Riya," Shivansh told her calmly, his voice tinged with a mix of regret and simmering rage.

"We were being compromised. Someone overtrumped us, due to the leakage of intel and set us up to fail."

Riya's jaw tightened as she met his gaze.

"Who do you think it was? Someone inside? Someone high up or someone whom we're fighting with?"

Shivansh didn't respond immediately, his mind racing through the possibilities.

"It has to be someone with access and he is working within the team with us. Someone who knew the operation details of ours. And the way they coordinated—" he paused, his thoughts darkening, "this isn't an amateur work. They want to cripple us and send us the message that they're at least two steps ahead of us anytime, every time."

Riya's lips curled into a bitter smile. "Not entirely. They might walk away clean, but we rattle them. No one puts this much effort into misdirection unless they're protecting something bigger. Plus, we capture their leader, who's seriously injured. This could be an internal signal, triggering a shift in their power dynamics. Otherwise, why would they leave their leader injured and in our custody? It doesn't make sense."

Shivansh gave a slight nod, his resolve hardened. "The Scorpion," he said, his tone sharp. "They use it to bait us, but its real purpose remains unchanged. Whatever they're moving is important enough to risk exposure. They think we're licking our wounds, but we're far from done. Let's interrogate the captured leader—I doubt he's the real kingpin."

Riya sat up straighter, her fiery determination returning. "We need to hit them back harder through this guy. They think we're compromised. Let's play their game. Feed them false leads, force them into the open."

 Shivansh's eyes gleamed with a renewed sense of purpose. "Exactly. We'll use the injured leader as bait. Make them believe we've extracted valuable information out of him. They'll scramble to cover their tracks and that's when we'll strike."

The room buzzed with a newfound energy as Shivansh and Riya laid out their plan. They would orchestrate a series of controlled leaks, false information designed to sow confusion and panic within the enemy ranks. The Narcotics Bureau would carefully craft each piece of false information to lure the traffickers into its traps.

"We need to coordinate with our tech team," Riya said, pulling up a list of contacts. "They can plant the false intel and monitor the enemy's communications. If they take the bait, we'll know immediately."

Shivansh nodded, his mind already several steps ahead. "We'll also need undercover agents to observe their reactions on the ground. If they start making moves, we need to be ready to intercept."

As they finalized their strategy, the tension in the air transformed into a palpable sense of anticipation. This was more than a counterattack; it was a chess game and Shivansh and Riya were determined to outmanoeuvre their opponents.

The interrogation room was prepared and the captured leader was brought in, his wounds bandaged but his spirit unbroken. Shivansh leaned in, his voice low and menacing. "You're going to help us, whether you want to or not. Your people left you behind and now you're going to pay the price."

The man's eyes flickered with defiance, but Shivansh could see the fear beneath the surface. "We're going to feed you just enough truth to make your lies believable," he continued. "And you're going to play your part. Because if you don't, I promise you, things will get very uncomfortable for you."

Riya watched from the corner, her eyes sharp and unyielding. She knew this was their best chance to turn the tide. The leader's hesitation, his uncertainty, would be their weapon.

Hours later, as the operation unfolded, the first pieces of false intel were released that the captured leader started revealing the operation. The shadowy corridors of power and deceit would be exposed and justice would be served sooner. Within minutes, they began to see results. Enemy communications spiked, filled with frantic attempts to verify the information. Moves were made and the Bureau's traps began to close in.

As the night wore on, Shivansh and Riya remained vigilant, tracking every development. The real masterminds were still out there, but for the first time, they had the upper hand. They were no longer just reacting; they were dictating the terms of engagement.

Shivansh glanced at Riya; his resolve unwavering. "We'll take them down, one by one. Until there's nothing left. However, ensure the life threat for the witness."

Riya nodded, her eyes filled with determination. "Let's finish this."

Shivansh allowed himself a small, grim smile. "If they think they're the only ones who can play dirty, they're in for a surprise. First, we track down the leak. Then we dismantle their operation piece by piece. Let's talk with the guy again in the hospital tomorrow."

"Get some rest," Shivansh finally told Riya, though his own body screamed for the same. "We've got work to do. And this time, we're the ones setting the trap."

Riya nodded, her gaze steely. "We'll make them regret underestimating us." Riya left the room to rest.

The next day, the room fell silent for a moment, the weight of their losses hanging heavy in the air. Yet beneath it was an undercurrent of unyielding determination. They were bruised, battered and grieving, but they weren't broken. The battle wasn't over—it was only at the beginning.

INTERROGATION
CHAPTER-6

Chapter 6: The Interrogation

"Arjun Sinha," Shivansh said coldly, pressing his gun to the man's temple at the interrogation room.

"We again meet."

Sinha's defiant look met Shivansh's. "Do you think arresting me will change anything? The myth is already out there. You're just fighting a lost war, Inspector."

Shivansh leaned forward, his voice low and threatening. "We've taken down bigger players than you, Sinha. Start talking, or things will get very uncomfortable for you."

Sinha chuckled coldly and mirthlessly. "You truly don't understand it, do you? We have already moved. We're everywhere now. You cut off one head, and two more will grow in its place. It's the same as Hydra's head. Have you read Greek mythology?"

Riya, who had been silently observing, eventually spoke. "Who is the mastermind behind this movement?" Sinha, you are just a puppet. "Who is pulling your strings?"

Sinha's sneer disappeared, leaving behind a calculated expression. "You will never find him out. But you'll notice the results soon enough."

The man sneered and laughed as the handcuffs were fastened around his wrists. "You have lost this round, Inspector. You are always the loser. You don't know who you're fighting with. First of all, my name is Rajesh, not Sinha. I just work for him. You don't even know him either and you can't even reach him; he's a big fry. You squandered the opportunity in Haldia twenty years ago. You stayed the same fool, and now you are unable to reach him. You have merely scratched the surface. You can't keep me here for long because you don't have evidence. "My lawyer is on his way to court."

Shivansh's grip tightened around the handcuffs as a wave of frustration and anger washed over him. The mention of Haldia was a raw nerve, a reminder of a botched operation that had haunted him for years.

"But how did he learn about it? *Was he present? What is a "myth"?* - Shivansh felt embarrassed because there were so many unanswered questions.

Rajesh's words stung, reopening old wounds. Shivansh's eyes hardened, the memories fuelling his resolve.

"You think this is over, Rajesh? You're wrong. We've learned from our mistakes. Sinha may be out of reach for now, but we'll find him soon. And as for you," he leaned in closer, his voice a dangerous whisper,

"Don't you think you've told us enough? Even if you don't tell us anything, they'll find you sooner than we do. Because if you believe a lawyer can protect you from what is coming, you are more delusional than I believed. They will terminate you sooner or later; you have two options: leave and risk being killed or stay with us and speak; we will protect you because we have already spread the word that you have begun to disclose information to us. Think about it. The choice is yours."

Riya stepped forward, her presence a steadying force. "We're not the same team you ambushed in Haldia years ago. We've grown stronger, smarter. And we have you now, Rajesh. You're a loose end and loose ends get tied up. We will open that case now."

Rajesh's smirk faltered for a moment, but he quickly regained his composure. "You'll get nothing from me. Sinha is untouchable; even I don't know him well. You're wasting your time."

But Shivansh saw the flicker of doubt in Rajesh's eyes, the crack in his defiant facade. "We'll see about that," he said, straightening up.

"Take him to the court. Make sure he's comfortable. We're going to be here for a while."

As Rajesh was led away, Shivansh turned to Riya. "We need to dig deeper. Sinha's network is vast, but it's not impenetrable. Rajesh is a smart as@#le. We'll break him if we get a chance, but this time we can't hold him because we have nothing and when we do that, we'll follow the trail all the way to Sinha. Keep your eyes on him and give him protection. Open the Haldia case against him."

Riya nodded, her expression resolute. "We'll get them, Sir. One by one, we'll dismantle their empire."

Shivansh's eyes burned with determination. "For Haldia. For every time they've slipped through my fingers. We'll bring them down and we'll do it together."

Riya left to take Rajesh to the court. Shivansh Rathore walked down to the parking for his SUV.

Frustrated but undeterred, Shivansh and Riya left the interrogation room. They had enough to hold, but the elusive puppet master remained out of reach.

Rajesh's words sent a chill through Shivansh. This wasn't just about smuggling—it was about something called "Myth" maybe more related to power, control or something far more insidious. The implications of Rajesh's statement hung in the air, thick with the promise of an escalating war.

As the SUV started the flash back of Haldia came to his mind

Flashback to Haldia, Ten Years Ago

The docks of Haldia were bathed in the eerie glow of floodlights, casting long shadows across the stacks of shipping containers. Shivansh and his team moved with practiced stealth, the tension palpable as they approached their target. The intel had been solid— or so they thought. This was supposed to be the raid that brought down Arjun Sinha, a rising figure in the criminal underworld. Shivansh was just a young entrant in the field and that was his first field operation on behalf of NCB. His boss banked on Shivansh's calibre as a rookie and asked him to lead the mission independently.

The plan had seemed airtight. They had the location, the timing and the element of surprise. But as they

moved in, a deafening explosion tore through the night, throwing Shivansh off his feet. The blast was followed by a hail of gunfire and chaos erupted. The smell of burning debris filled the air, mingling with the sharp tang of gunpowder. The similar deceptions, the similar actors.

Shivansh scrambled to his feet, his ears ringing from the explosion. The scene before him was chaos—his team caught in a vicious firefight, bullets whizzing through the air, the acrid smell of gunpowder thick around them. The ambush had been perfectly orchestrated, a devastating counterstrike that left them reeling. Amid the smoke and confusion, Arjun Sinha had slipped through their grasp, leaving behind a scene of destruction and loss.

In the midst of the chaos, Shivansh's gaze fell upon a young dock worker, injured and terrified. The boy's eyes met his, wide with fear and determination. For a moment, Shivansh hesitated, wondering if this boy could be Sinha or Rajesh. How could he be there? If he had orchestrated the blast, why was he wounded and stranded? He could have also fled with his team. Or that was also the same deception?

But the immediacy of the firefight pulled Shivansh's focus back to his team. The boy was forgotten in the heat of the moment, yet that image of fear and determination lingered in his mind. The aftermath was a blur of sirens and stretcher-bearers, the wounded being rushed to hospitals.

Shivansh had stood amidst the wreckage, the weight of failure heavy on his shoulders. Haldia was supposed to be their victory, a decisive strike against Sinha's empire. Instead, it had turned into a nightmare, a catastrophic failure that had cost them dearly.

Shivansh was left to take the entire responsibility for the operation's failure. The media had a field day and higher-ups demanded explanations. The blame settled squarely on his shoulders, marking the beginning of a long, arduous path of redemption that Shivansh walked so far.

@dibyenduchoudhury

Chapter 7:
Delhi Call

Chapter 7: Delhi Call (Four days after the Kamarajar Operation)

The following day of the port raid, it made headlines and sparked multiple conversations on national television. The public was made aware of the massive raid and failure, but the deeper layers of the scheme were kept secret, known only to law enforcement officials. Even Rajesh's bail was kept under wraps. However, the loss of so many lives sparked outrage. Everyone resented Shivansh Rathore for his foreboding decision and for exposing his failures.

Shivansh and Riya worked tirelessly, poring over files, tracking financial records and interrogating Sinha's other associates. Each clue they uncovered painted a more disturbing picture of a network that was deeply embedded in the geopolitical fabric of multiple nations. The difficulty of their undertaking was enormous, yet their determination remained unwavering. However, Sinha or any of his close associates would not be held back to prison for further queries because of the absence of any "illegal activities/acts" that could be backed by evidence. Even Rajesh had gone missing since leaving court on bail.

Riya came across a link late one night while going through a particularly detailed collection of financial documents, which sparked warning lights. "Look at this, sir." All transfers go from a Singaporean shell company to an Indian political fund. And it's linked to another account in Dubai. Shivansh's eyes squinted as he examined the documents. "This isn't simply about smuggling or money laundering. They are buying influence to protect their operations at the highest levels.

Their investigation led them further into a network of corruption and power dynamics that went far beyond the ports and narcotics. They discovered connections to human trafficking rings, money laundering operations, and potentially terrorist financing. The scope of the plot was breathtaking, and the stakes were larger than they had ever imagined.

Despite the rising strain and risk that came with each new discovery, Shivansh and Riya persevered. They recognized that dismantling this operation would require more than just tenacity but also strategic brilliance and unwavering determination. The situation has to be pushed to higher-ups in Delhi.

Late that evening, as they examined the day's data in a dimly lit office, Shivansh could feel the weight of the upcoming struggle.

Papers were strewn around the desk, and the room was filled with the sound of printers and computers processing prints and data. The fragrance of stale coffee clung in the air, a monument to their long working hours. Despite the ongoing tiredness and anxiety, Shivansh felt a fresh sense of purpose. They were not simply fighting a drug war in NCB; it appears that they were battling for the very essence of their country. The understanding that their efforts had the potential to influence their country's destiny gave them the motivation to continue.

Riya looked up from her laptop, her eyes full of purpose. "We're getting closer, Sir. Every day, we peel away another layer. They cannot hide eternally. However, I believe the NCB is too little to handle this issue."

Shivansh nodded, his determination strengthened. "We will not stop until every link in the network is severed and every shady figure is exposed. The war is far from ended, but each step brings us closer to justice. The hands of justice are long enough to handle this situation.

Their next move involved coordinating with international agencies. They needed to track the flow of money and goods across borders and this required a concerted effort from multiple countries and multiple agencies within India. Every conversation, every shared piece of information, was a step towards tightening the noose around the syndicate; however, it was difficult to pursue the same within the limit of NCB.

A call rang in his phone; "Yes, Madam," he said, and hung up with a smile for Riya. Shivansh was working on gaining access with Nair Madam in the background because he knew some time ago that the entire web is much greater than NCB's capacity to digest and he had been connected with some time, sharing all inputs with her that Riya was unaware of until now.

"Riya, with all these papers, we need to go to Delhi tomorrow. A phone call came from the Ministry of External Affairs. The meeting is there tomorrow morning at 10:00 am. I'll get the tickets now and related approvals; you get these papers with you." He left the room with a smile for a cigarette.

As they prepared for the next phase of their Delhi trip, the horizon of Chennai began to glow with the first light of dawn. The city was waking up to a new day, unaware of the silent battles fought to keep it safe. Shivansh and Riya stood to catch the morning flight for Delhi at Chennai International Airport in Tirusulam.

Chapter-8
CONSPIRACY THEORY
@dibyenduchoudhury

Chapter 8: Conspiracy Theory

In the Ministry of External Affairs, tensions were running high in the RAW Headquarters. Foreign Secretary Kavita Iyer was in the war room, surrounded by intelligence officials from the NSA, CBI, Navy and senior diplomats. Maps of the Indian Ocean region were pinned on the walls, marked with red circles and dotted lines, each one with a potential threat point.

"The pattern is very much clear," she said, her voice was sharp and unwavering. "Pakistan's ISI and China's MSS are not just facilitating all of this for nothing; they're up to something and trying to make something bigger or establishing a route for trafficking weapons and financial warfare against us. Their goal is to destabilize India from within. First, Kashmir, then Punjab and the Northeast of India and now they are targeting South India. We cannot allow this new route to solidify to destabilize India."

Representing the NCB were Shivansh and Riya, while Aarav was presenting the Navy. Kavita Iyer scanned through all the documents Shivansh brought and addressed the room, her gaze fixed on Shivansh.

"Though you've been recommended to hand over the charge to someone subordinate to you and to be transferred to another location because of your goof-up at Kamarajar Port, I brought you to Delhi to lead the Special Operation Team reporting to me in parallel to your boss at NCB, staying at Chennai and the name of this special operation team is "Gelisko" because it seems there's an old relationship you have with Sinha since Haldia and an old account to be settled. I am offering you a lifeline, Shivansh, to either settle the score with him or resign from here." She told him in a very cutthroat manner, openly.

"Why Gelisko? Many may ask. "She continued

"War horses serve as a metaphor for the team's name, Gelisko, which stands for strength, endurance, adaptability, and grace. Each member is handpicked for their particular skills and resilience and they are expected to face obstacles with grace and resolve. The team is based on mutual trust and a common dedication to the objective, with each member's duty being to explore unexplored territory, innovate, and lead courageously. Any questions?"

No one asked any questions, as is customary. The room was buzzing with urgency as analysts shared updates. The aroma of hot coffee filled the air, as did the hum of strained conversations. Every bit of intelligence was exchanged, which might be a game changer, and national security could not be more important.

"Unrest between tribal communities on the Andaman and Nicobar Islands is escalating," one officer reported. His voice was tight, indicating the tension of constant watching.

"We believe it's being fuelled by paid agitators to distract local authorities."

Another ambassador added, "Unrest looks to be growing in Bangladesh, with the goal of toppling the current government. Fundamentalist groups appear to be supporting this campaign, which is likely part of a wider agenda. The purpose is to establish and control a critical shipping route, which is a key component in this power play. We have reason to suspect that Pakistan's intelligence service, the ISI, is actively helping this operation. The ISI's involvement in this strategic corridor could significantly impact regional trade and geopolitics, potentially creating instability in South Asia. This aligns with extremists' planned strategy to exploit

Bangladesh's vulnerabilities, potentially causing prolonged instability."

Kavita's eyes narrowed as she processed the information. "We need a multi-pronged approach," she suggested, her voice remained steady but intense.

"Coordinate with the Bureau and inform the Navy. We need boots on the ground and eyes in the sky. If this route is established, we're not just dealing with a small problem like terrorism in Kashmir; this time they definitely have a bigger agenda. We're looking at a gateway for terrorism, arms smuggling, drugs and civil unrest."

A young intelligence officer approached Kavita with a classified document. "Ma'am, we are receiving satellite images showing unusual maritime activity near the Andaman Sea. It can be a rendezvous point for the next shipment from Myanmar."

Kavita scanned the document; her expression remained grim. She told Aarav, "Get this to Naval Command ASAP. Increase patrols in that area and use our reconnaissance drones. If there is a rendezvous, we need to keep an eye on it.

The atmosphere in the room became even more intense. Kavita took a minute to gather herself before addressing the audience: "I can anticipate a coordinated campaign to destabilize our nation.

However, we will answer with equal coordination and resolve. Utilize all resources. This concludes here."

With that, the room erupted in controlled mayhem. Officers and diplomats travelled with purpose, their roles delineated in the vast network of defense and intelligence operations. The fight against the shadow war began, and its devious allies formed a multi-headed beast ready to attack at any head.

Aarav, representing the Navy, spoke up. "Our naval patrols are ready to increase their presence in the Andaman Sea, Madam. We'll deploy additional reconnaissance drones to monitor suspicious maritime activity."

Kavita nodded, happy with the prompt reaction. "And we must notify our international allies. This network has spread beyond our borders, necessitating a coordinated effort to destroy it. Create a brief for each of our embassies and request information on unusual activities in their respective areas."

As the conference progressed, the chamber buzzed with the urgency of a war council. Officers and diplomats collaborated, with duties well defined in the vast network of defense and intelligence activities. Every detail was studied, and every possible lead was pursued.

As she exited the war room, Kavita couldn't help but consider the larger consequences. She was prepared to brief the National Security Meeting, which the Prime Minister of India was presiding over.

She knew it wasn't simply about blocking a cargo, apprehending a few important people, or killing a few terrorists through surgical strikes within their domain; they were now approaching and encircling them.

This was about ensuring the stability and future of the country. The road ahead was riddled with difficulties, but she was confident they had the courage and resilience to triumph.

Outside, the city of Delhi was shrouded in darkness till the next day. Kavita took a deep breath and braced herself for the long fight ahead. She recognized that success would not come from a single battle, but from continuous pursuit and unshakable dedication, with several sacrifices ahead. Even if this war is not resolved today, it will last beyond her lifetime. Every move, every approach, represented a step toward guaranteeing the country's future.

Chapter-9
The
Boundaries
Blurred
@dibyenduchoudhury

Chapter 9: The Boundaries Blurred

The final flight back to Chennai from Delhi was cancelled due to an unforeseen technical issue before passengers could board it. Tickets for the next morning were handed to Shivansh and Riya with others and plans were made for them to stay at a nearby hotel with a free dinner by the airliner. As they acclimatized to the hotel, the fatigue from their demanding previous few days was evident. Shivansh and Riya were thankful for the unexpectedly extended time together out of the office, even though the travel cancellation was inconvenient. They talked about all the discussions they had with other team members while they were in Delhi as they ate dinner and the forthcoming operations. Although the lines separating personal and professional ties had gotten increasingly hazy, it didn't seem to matter at that time. They simply enjoyed one another's company and were glad to be together, even discussing their family.

After dinner, Riya accompanied Shivansh to his room. They had been through so much together since the Kamarajar Port operation and the weight of the day's events hung heavily in the air with a new operation named "Gelisko."

Shivansh sat back on his couch and closed his eyes for a moment of calm. Riya sat on the bed, facing him, her presence a soothing reminder that they had survived the trauma together and were still alive.

The room was peaceful, with the only sound being the distant buzz of airport-bound traffic and airport activities. Shivansh opened his eyes and looked at Riya, who was staring out the window at the airport lights.

"It has been a long day," he said softly. Riya turned to Shivansh and nodded in accord. "But we made it this far," she said, her voice overflowing with thankfulness for the opportunity. Shivansh reached out and squeezed her hand gently. They sat on the bed in silence for a short while, enjoying each other's company. The city lights continued to flicker outside.

Riya looked to Shivansh, her expression a mix of exhaustion and relief. "It's been a long day, but I build my life around it since every day isn't like today. I am very delighted and grateful to you."

A pleasant silence fell between them. Riya appreciated his assistance not only today, but throughout the endeavor. The link they had built was unmistakable and it had grown stronger with each hardship they encountered. However, Riya never anticipated that Shivansh would give her access to such a wider platform because she was well aware that in the government, bosses can easily obtain such credits and never share them with their subordinates.

 "Riya," Shivansh began, his voice gentle, "Please, do not think I am doing any favour to you; in reality, I don't know what I would have done without you. Your support means a lot to me." He paused and then continued, "You know, at one point when they took you away to the hospital after the blast, I was suddenly feeling that I lost you."

Riya smiled softly. "You've been my rock, Sir; we make a good team. I'm back here."

The exhaustion began to catch up with them as the night cuddled deeper. Shivansh stood up and stretched, looking at the clock. "It's getting late. We should get some rest. The flight is in a few hours."

Riya nodded, but she didn't get up to go to her room. Rather, she gave him a gaze of passion that surprised him.

"I need to tell you something. You have my heartfelt gratitude for the attention you gave after the blast. Without you, Mahi would have been left as an orphan. I'm the only person he has. Thank you for being there for both of us." Riya told, her voice filled with emotion.

Shivansh was shocked by her comments, and he felt a wave of warmth in his chest. "I will do anything for you and Mahi within my means; please be assured," he said, reaching out to take her hands again. For a minute, they sat silently side by side on the bed, the weight of their shared memories hanging in the air.

Recognizing the gravity of what she had spoken, he resumed his position facing her. "Riya, what is it?" He was aware that Riya was parenting her disabled son alone after divorcing within two years of their marriage. She ended her marriage to her batchmate, which was quite difficult. He was also an NCB officer in the class of 2000. Riya was in her early thirties and had been juggling work, parenting, and her personal life with grace and determination.

She took a deep breath, gathered her thoughts. "I know things are not complicated between us, probably the rumours about us complicate your married life. The way we're constantly balancing our professional and personal lives—it's overwhelming.

But I need you to know that I care about you, probably more than I should."

The air between them seemed to crackle with unspoken words. Slowly, almost tentatively, Riya reached out and took his hand. "Shivansh, I don't want to lose what we have. But I also don't want to keep pretending that I don't feel something more."

His thoughts were racing as he gave her hand a light squeeze. He was aware of the dangers and the boundaries, but right then, all he could think about was how much she meant to him and how he could comfort her. He told in a lighter tone

"Riya, do not worry much; we'll deal with whatever comes up together. I swear. I'll look after Mahi as well."

A wave of comfort swept over Riya as Shivansh's words took hold. She knew she was venturing into uncharted territory then. Shivansh was married and had a daughter. His wife, Swapna, whom Riya knew very well, was envious of her. Riya was aware that she was drowning, but drowning had its own allure. Her heart had felt weak for Shivansh for a long time and she had thought about this close moment with Shivansh countless times before. Every time she had the strength to stop the thinking further, but tonight she didn't find that power in herself, nor was she interested either.

She was aware that their lives would become more complex. But the magic was present in that moment; all she could feel was a deep sense of connection and longing. Shivansh's commitment to watch after her son, Mahi, struck a deep chord with her. It reflected the type of man he was responsible, caring, and totally committed to those he loved. Despite the upheaval and uncertainty, Riya sensed a glimmer of hope. Because of their combined strength and determination, they were able to effectively traverse the turbulent waters ahead. Their route was riddled with difficulties, but Riya felt prepared to face whatever lay ahead of her, thanks to Shivansh's calming presence. The allure of their link, as perilous as it was, gave her the strength to venture into the unknown, believing that they would find a way through together.

She leaned in and became much closer, her eyes searching his for reassurance before diving in deep. "Do you really mean what you just said?"

Shivansh, aware of the challenges in his personal life, remained unwavering despite personal strains and rumours of an affair. He understood relationships are complex and not always defined by conventional standards. His commitment to his family extended beyond physical presence, providing emotional support and hope for peace lately.

"Yes," he whispered, his voice barely audible. "I mean it."

"Already the worst had happened to me without compromising my professional relationship with Riya; what else could happen?" he told himself. *"Infidelity, breach of loyalty—how does it matter if in reality I get those feelings from someone else? He is also a human being and he deserves love, respects and all."*

Their relationship had been built over the last few years on mutual respect and love and Shivansh believed that the foundation was strong enough to withstand this storm, though they have a huge age difference. He longed for the day when Swapna would look past the gossip and see the truth in his eyes.

Yet, as he sat beside Riya, their hands intertwined, the connection he felt with her was undeniable. Far more complicated situations Shivansh navigated so far with a clear mind. He knew the importance of maintaining boundaries, yet he couldn't help but feel the warmth and comfort that Riya provided.

Without another word, Riya closed the distance between them, her lips finding his in a tender, lingering kiss. The world outside faded away, leaving only the two of them, lost in a moment that felt both inevitable and surreal.

As they pulled away, breathless and slightly dazed, Shivansh looked into Riya's eyes and saw the same mix of emotions he felt—hope, fear and a deep connection that blurred their professional and age boundaries.

That night, they crossed a line that should never be uncrossed. Their professional boundaries blurred and they found comfort in each other's arms. It was a moment of weakness, but also a moment of undeniable attraction and connection that existed as basic instincts in men. Both the body tried to sink into each other with care and love on the bed on that night with no further ado.

After a few hours, Shivansh was wracked with guilt, knowing that his wife, Swapna, would never understand this neither mercy him forever. The rumours about his affair with Riya had already strained their marriage and this momentary weakness of the last night would only make things worse.

Riya, too, was conflicted. She valued her professional relationship with Shivansh and feared that their personal entanglement would jeopardize everything they had worked for. But despite the complications, neither of them could deny the bond they shared. Their relationship became a delicate dance at that point, a balancing act between their professional duties and their personal feelings that were overriding each other. Their connection had grown stronger with each passing minute. Both of them longed for that which was completely missing in their lives. Both were thirsty for something real and genuine for a long time. They both knew that they had found it in each other.

They were acutely aware that their journey ahead remained uncertain and fate might never allow them to reach a destination together. However, sometimes we also enjoy just our journey without any destination too. Each one, in this intricate journey of their fate, could only afford to give comfort and intimacy to the other. Achieving a joint destination probably was a utopian dream. Yet, they were determined to explore their luck together. It was never necessary to have name to every relationship either.

On their return flight, Shivansh and Riya did not say anything to each other. Riya leaned on Shivansh's shoulder, holding his right arm close to her chest and looking out the window at the sky. She wanted to enjoy every moment of her presence and closeness with him, showing her intimacy and dependency during their flight like a swan. The swan of her thoughts soared off last night for a risky and unknown destination.

They were aware that their future was uncertain, but Shivansh and Riya were ready to face it hand in hand, drawing strength from their shared moments and the unwavering support they provided to each other. Their journey might be fraught with obstacles, but they were determined to make the most of their time together, no matter where fate would eventually lead them.

Chapter-10
The Spider's Web
@dibyenduchoudhury

Chapter 10: The Spider's Web

The house stood in the shadow of the bustling Colombo harbour, an unassuming edifice nestled among the urban sprawls. Its facade disguised the modest inside; all modern facilities were available inside, which contrasted with the poor appearance of its exterior in this region near the harbour. However, a storm was brewing beneath its modest roof, due to a guy whose serene appearance belied a mind filled with malicious intent.

A single desk lamp inside the room provided dimmer lighting, casting a golden glow over a large mahogany table in the centre. The polished surface reflected the cold light of Arjun Sinha's laptop screen, where he sat with his fingers flying across the keyboard. The faint hum of ships unloading cargo in the distance creates a symphony of secrecy and disorder. The room itself was a tribute to a man of intellect and contradiction. Wall-to-wall bookshelves framed the room, their hefty oak frames groaning under the weight of numerous books. Leather-bound volumes on philosophy, economics, and international trade were displayed alongside popular spy novels and texts in languages ranging from Mandarin to Russian. It was the collection of a man who valued both knowledge and dishonesty. Arjun landed at his house in Colombo, Sri Lanka, early in the morning to finish his operation and spend some time under the carpet.

Arjun leaned back in his chair, his sharp eyes scanning the laptop screen for encrypted messages. The shifting light highlighted his face's sharp angles, which conveyed neither fear nor doubt. He was deep in thought, checking data points, reviewing ship manifests, and finishing the details of an international transaction. A half-empty tumbler of whiskey sat to his right, its amber liquid glinting faintly in the light. A sheaf of papers lay laid out beside it, including maps of the Indian Ocean, lists of coded coordinates, and a photograph of the M.V. Orion, a cargo vessel. Each document was a piece of Arjun's vast puzzle, a covert operation that straddled the line between legality and chaos. Every keystroke on the laptop was deliberate, and each move was planned. Arjun was not someone who took risks. Precision, to him, was linked with power, which meant everything.

As he worked, a faint vibration resonated across the table. The screen showed an important notification. Arjun's brow wrinkled as he opened the mail. It arrived from one of his trusty operatives: a coded notification about strange surveillance activity near the Kerala Port. His lips make a tiny line.

"So," he said, barely audible. "They've started sniffing around."

Unfazed, he closed the laptop and stood up. He went to the bookshelf and got a faded atlas. A satellite phone was buried within the hollowed-out pages. Arjun dialled a number, and the line connected with a sequence of encrypted beeps. Moments later, a voice crackled across the line: "What's the matter, boss?" On the other side was Javed, who stood by the pier and watched the activity.

Arjun's eyebrows tightened as he said, "We must speed our plans. "They're on us."

"We have a problem," he remarked calmly but firmly. "Implement countermeasures immediately. Increase security at the Kerala docks. Moving the Scorpion to contingency route B is also being studied. I want all details handled—no loose ends."

He stopped the call and put the phone back in its hiding place. Arjun went back to his desk and poured himself another glass of whiskey, swirling it thoughtfully. The game became more intense. The soldiers were closing in, but Arjun was not a man who cowered in the face of peril. He lived and thrived within it, spinning plans and counterplans like a spider in a web.

As he took a slow sip, his gaze wandered to the bookcases. The wisdom of generations surrounded him, yet it was his own cunning and ruthlessness that had gotten him here. Outside, the port continued its never-ending activity, oblivious to the guy in the home, plotting an operation that could change the balance of power across borders. The primary entry into the harbour remained well guarded, with security officials strategically stationed. Throughout the property, surveillance cameras monitored employee, truck, and freight movements. The port was a well-oiled machine that performed with near-perfect precision and efficiency. It was made difficult for both locals and unauthorised visitors to enter this region.

A massive control tower loomed over the docks, like a sentinel. From this vantage point, controllers could monitor the whole complex and coordinate ship and container movements with military precision. The tower was outfitted with cutting-edge technology, including radar systems, satellite communications, and complicated computer networks.

Beyond the warehouses, a network of railways and roads connected the port to the rest of the region's infrastructure. This link was critical to the port's strategic importance since it enabled the rapid transportation of commodities across borders and into the heart of marketplaces. The highways were jam-packed with trucks, each transporting merchandise to and from the port with maximum efficiency.

The port's construction had not been without controversy in Sri Lankan history. Local residents had been displaced, and environmental concerns had been raised, but the project proceeded with the full support of the Chinese government. For them, the port was more than just a trading hub; it was a strategic foothold, a symbol of their rising worldwide power as part of their geopolitical expansion strategy. Under the pretence of friendly cooperation in higher interests, Arjun helped a number of participants arrange a loan of several billion dollars to the country and government officials. Now that the country's situation had changed with a new government, Arjun remained in his safe haven within the port area, despite the fact that his allies in the former government were also present, whom he avoided in the current setting.

He relished the invincibility and inaccessibility to any power of the world at that point. The phone received an SMS that disturbed Arjun's thoughts from some unknown number, which seldom happened because his Sri Lankan number was available with the selected few.

The message simply read, "I know where you are hiding." Arjun's heart raced as he realized that his safe haven might not be as secure as he had believed. He quickly began to reassess his situation and consider his next move. Was that "Shivansh Rathore?"

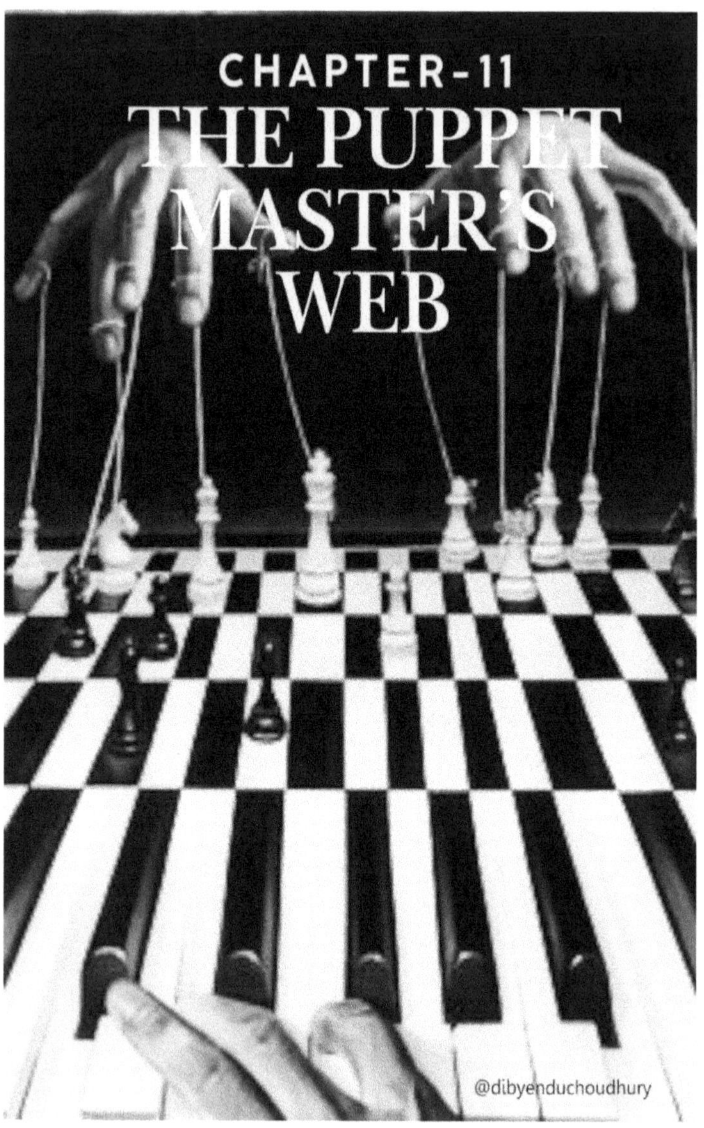
CHAPTER-11
THE PUPPET
MASTER'S
WEB
@dibyenduchoudhury

Chapter 11: The Puppet Master's Web

Arjun rose from the couch and moved to a wall lined with floor-to-ceiling bookcases. With a flick of his wrist, he opened a leather-bound book to reveal a secret safe. Inside, there was a satellite phone, several types of untraceable SIM cards, and a small stack of encrypted USB sticks.

He pulled one out, plugged it into his secured laptop and opened a series of surveillance feeds. Grainy footage from ports, warehouses and clandestine meetings flickered across the screen. Each frame was a piece of a puzzle only he could see.

"This isn't just about one shipment, Javed," Arjun said, his voice calm but menacing. "This is about maintaining the route. This is just the beginning and Myth must hit the market of India. Once we control the corridor, we'll own this trade—not just drugs but weapons, people and influence. And that kind of power? It's untouchable."

Javed nodded, but the unease in his eyes didn't escape Arjun's notice. Tell Shiraz, your brother, to sail to Gwadar Port and layover for some days at Pakistan in the Arabian Sea and leave Kochi right now. We have no other choice. We will have to find a suitable time and opportunity to unload it some other time in a different way.

He sent a text through his mobile to a number. Arjun redirected his focus to the laptop screen, monitoring the broadcasts with hungry intent. He could see dockworkers moving containers, discreet exchanges in dimly lit warehouses, and secret meetings held at night. Each sight was a tribute to the massive global network he had established, one that relied on secrecy and precision in every port in Southeast Asia.

"Every piece is in place, Javed." Arjun said with a deliberate tone. "We've got the logistics, supply chains, and people. The Bureau and RAW believe they can disrupt us, but they are playing catch-up game right now. By the time they understand and act, we'll have moved on to the next stage."

Javed shifted his weight, still displaying suspicion. "But what if they can intercept another shipment coming from Myanmar right now by fishing boat? "What if they get closer than we expect?"

Arjun's expression stiffened. "Then we'll adjust again. We have faced dangers before and emerged stronger. Our edge lies in our capacity to alter tactics quickly. Make sure all of our operatives are on high alert. Check all of our routes and make any necessary contingency preparations. I want no margin for error."

He waited to allow his words to sink in. The room was quiet save for the faint hum of the laptop and the distant murmur of the port.

"And Javed," Arjun added, his voice taking on a sharper edge, "keep an eye on our inside sources. If anyone shows signs of wavering, just eliminate them. We cannot afford to have any leaks."

Javed's eyes widened slightly, but he nodded. "Understood, sir. I'll handle it. It seems Rajesh talked more in his captivity to Rathore."

Arjun watched as Javed left the room, the door closing softly behind him. He turned back to the laptop, the surveillance feeds now showing a new set of images—potential allies, rival cartels and international contacts. The scope of his operation was immense, spanning continents and involving some of the world's most dangerous players.

He reached for the satellite phone and dialled a secure number. "Activate Project Eclipse," he said tersely. "I want all units ready to move at a moment's notice. Inform our contacts in Bangladesh and Myanmar to prepare for the next wave."

The voice on the other end acknowledged the order and Arjun hung up, his mind already racing ahead. Project Eclipse was one of his most ambitious plans, designed to consolidate his power and expand his influence even further to make the country destabilize as part of the "Deep State Theory." It involved not just smuggling but also strategic alliances, ruling the government from the backdoor for the calculated betrayals. He grinned slightly.

As he sat back in his chair, Arjun allowed himself a rare moment of satisfaction. He had built an empire from the shadows and now he was poised to take it to new heights. The night deepened and the city of Colombo was getting slow from its usual rhythm. Arjun's thoughts were already on the next move, the next deal, the next conquest. His ambition was boundless, his resolve unbreakable. Arjun's mind raced as he sat in the room after Javed left, the weight of the revelation pressing down on him.

Arjun was aware of Javed and Rajesh's internal squabbles and rivalry, but he dismissed them as harmless competition. They had disputes, but betrayal? It appeared unfathomable. A knock on the door interrupted Arjun's thinking. Javed re-entered, his face filled with concern. "We need to talk," he added, his voice firm yet eager. Javed took a long breath and carefully selected his words. "Sorry, I came again. Last time, I wish I could tell you. The evidence, however, is damning. Last night, we intercepted a transmission carrying coded messages, which Rajesh only told Rathore about our Kerala plans. It is consistent with the information we obtained from our sources. He was returning to Andaman after his bail, but I had to..." Arjun's heart sank.

Arjun was aware of Javed and Rajesh's internal squabbles and rivalry, but he dismissed them as harmless competition. They had disputes, but betrayal? It appeared unfathomable.

A knock on the door interrupted Arjun's thinking. Javed re-entered, his face filled with concern. "We need to talk," he added, his voice firm yet eager. Javed took a long breath and carefully selected his words.

"Sorry, I came again. Last time, I wish I could tell you. The evidence, however, is damning. Last night, we intercepted a transmission carrying coded messages, which Rajesh only told Rathore about our Kerala plans. It is consistent with the information we obtained from our sources. He was returning to Andaman after his bail, but I had to..." Arjun's heart sank.

The puzzle pieces were coming into place, but he couldn't bring himself to accept them. "There needs to be an explanation. Maybe he was coerced, or perhaps someone is framing him."

Javed shook his head, his face sombre. "I thought about it all. The facts, however, are plain. Rajesh has been compromised and is informing them about our activities and plans."

The room went silent, with the seriousness of the situation hanging in the air. Arjun felt a flood of rage and betrayal rush over him. How could Rajesh, their brother-in-arms, turn against them? What may have motivated him to make such a decision?

Arjun nodded slowly, having made up his mind. "You're correct, Javed. Next time, before making such a decision, you should consult with me. We cannot allow personal feelings to impair our judgment. There's no room for traitors here. Remember, this might be Rathore's strategy to weaken us.

Rain began to fall in this part of the island country due to the overcast weather. This was a lovely country where tea and coffee could be produced at sea level due to the climate, but in India, steep terrains were required. A steady drumming against the window as Arjun and Javed braced themselves for what lay ahead. The unfathomable betrayal had led them to a crossroads and one of his closest advisers had been eliminated.

The voyage was far from done, and Arjun understood that the greatest test of loyalty and resilience was still ahead. He would tackle it full on, determined to find the truth and protect people he still cared about.

For Arjun Sinha, the game wasn't over.

Chapter - 12
The Deadly
Distraction

Chapter 12: The Deadly Distraction

Arjun closed his laptop and turned to Javed, locking his eyes with him straight, as his mind was already racing ahead.

"We'll give them what they want—a distraction. Leak the location of a decoy shipment, something small but convincing, so that they also remain happy. We will absorb some loss. Let them focus all their energy on that while we move the real cargo under their noses."

Javed's eyes lit up with admiration, his earlier tension replaced with a newfound respect.

"You're a genius, boss. I salute your brain."

"Just give them some cocaine in their hands, not Myth, so that they do not even understand the real threat." Arjun sounded absentminded. He also didn't smile. His expression remained stern; his eyes were cold and calculating.

"I'm a survivor, Javed, along with you guys. And in this game, survival is everything; only the fittest can survive, trust me."

He walked over to the wall of bookshelves once more, his fingers grazing the spines of leather-bound volumes. With a practiced motion, he pulled another book, revealing a hidden compartment. Inside was a detailed map of the trade routes they controlled, marked with red and blue pins indicating strategic points and recent disruptions.

"We'll use the decoy to test their response time and readiness in Kerala now." Arjun continued; his tone remained firm and forceful.

"I want to watch how quickly they mobilize, where they concentrate, and how much effort they put in. I'd like to know which routes they keep unattended. Our counterstrike will only be effective in their undefended territory because it is not yet appropriate to confront and engage in a faceoff; we also need to know our enemies; alone, Shivansh Rathore cannot cover all of India."

Javed nodded and scribbled notes in a notebook. "I will place the decoy in a high-traffic area. Something that will capture their attention and resources. So that they don't have to scratch their heads much."

Arjun's eyes shone with joy. "Good. Also, guarantee that our real shipment travels via the alternative route and arrives in Gwadar. We'll keep it under wraps for this very reason. It's less straightforward, but it's safe."

Javed hesitated for a moment, then spoke up. "What about our contacts within the Bureau? Should we feed them false information as well?"

Arjun's smirk returned. "Precisely. Give them just enough to believe that they've got a real lead. It will keep them off-guarded and chasing ghosts after Kamarajar. Meanwhile, our true operation will continue uninterrupted. I may also send the shipment to Chittagong from Gwadar because something is upcoming there too."

As Javed left to execute the plan, Arjun poured himself another glass of whiskey. He moved to the window, gazing out over the city of Colombo. The twinkling lights and distant hum of traffic were a stark contrast to the dark, meticulous strategy playing out in his mind in this port city.

He took a slow sip, savouring the burn of the whiskey as he contemplated the stakes. This wasn't just about outwitting Rathore. He was sure enough that Rathore alone cannot do much sitting at NCB. Even an integrated and coordinated effort cannot stop him now—it was about solidifying his power, establishing and ensuring his control over the corridor and further expanding his influence into new territories.

Arjun knew that each move in this game required precision and foresight. Any misstep could unravel their carefully constructed network. But he always thrived on such pressures in the past, the high-stakes nature of their operations always fuelled his determination and people liked him for that.

Already Javed left the room; another soft knock interrupted his thoughts. It was another local lieutenant, carrying a folder of documents.

"Sir, the latest intelligence reports," the man said, handing over the folder.

Arjun flipped through the pages, his mind absorbing the data with swift efficiency.

"Good. Continue monitoring the Bureau's movements here in Sri Lanka and update me immediately if there's any change. I feel we are operating safely in this Chinese port within this country. They can't access any intel from here. Still, just ensure it."

As his local lieutenant left, Arjun returned to his thoughts, the wheels of his mind turning with relentless focus. A gentle chime from Arjun's phone interrupted his present-day thoughts.

A message came from Lynda: "Thinking of you. Stay sharp. L."

He sighed, a mix of frustration and longing. Lynda was always a step ahead and she never let him forget it. As he drained the last sip of drink, Arjun made a silent vow. The next time they meet, it would be like allies or lovers. Their invisible bond seemed unbreakable. At that point, the grand chessboard of their clandestine world was getting reorganized and reshaping their lives.

The night wore on, followed by the evening, the sea's rhythmic whispers mingling with Arjun's thoughts. Lynda's shadow loomed large at every moment; however, Arjun was no stranger to those shadows. With a final, determined sip off his drink, Arjun set the glass down and returned to his desk.

In the world he inhabited, there were no guarantees—only calculated risks and strategic gambles were part and parcel of life. Arjun was always prepared to face whatever came his way. He had built his empire on a foundation of resilience, trust and intelligence and he was not about to let anyone tear it down.

Arjun's relationship with Lynda, the enigmatic Russian queen operating in Phuket, Thailand, was a complex one, though. They never thought to get married so far; however, his heart was undeniably with her. Though Lynda last time indicated to settle down, he always had doubts whether their life would anytime allow them to get settled. Uncertainty became a shadow of their successes. Their bond went deep beyond the transactional nature of her profession; it was rooted in love and unspoken understanding.

He recalled their last encounter vividly. Lynda had travelled with five stunning women to the Nicobar Islands to spend time with him on his birthday. He remained confused; even he doesn't remember his own birthday,

"How could she manage to find it?"

Last year they met at his beachfront villa, a private resort owned by him, where they could escape the chaos of their respective worlds. A major part of that resort he opened for the other tourists visiting Nicobar Island. Those days were filled with laughter, companionship and a brief respite from the ever-looming shadows of their lives.

Despite the dangers and uncertainties of his own life, Arjun found solace in those moments with Lynda. It was a reminder of humanity that still existed beneath the hardened exterior he had cultivated. As he gazed out at the horizon, he knew that no matter what the challenges ahead, he would draw strength from their connection and the memories they had created together.

Chapter-12
MEMORY REKINDLED
FOR LYNDA
@dibyenduchoudhury

Chapter 13: Memory rekindled for Lynda (A year before in flashback)

Arjun's thoughts wandered back to Lynda.

The night outside was humid, the salty tang of the sea drifting through the open balcony doors of Arjun Sinha's sprawling private villa on Nicobar Island, which had a private dockyard and sprawling greenery with a horse stable on one side and was open to tourists year-round as a luxurious resort on the other. With its enormous white marble and glass facade lit up by moonlight and a private dock, the resort gave the impression of being an opulent fortress. Only Arjun stays on this side with his people when he returns to the island on special occasions, either alone or with special visitors. Inside, however, the air was thick with ideas as Arjun leaned against the balustrade, a tumbler of ancient rum in hand. His acute mind was rarely sidetracked, but tonight was an exception.

Lynda was an important woman to Arjun. The so-called "Queen of Phuket" was more than just a figurehead for Russia's brothels; she was a force of beauty. Her beauty was captivating, her intelligence razor-sharp, and her ruthlessness unparalleled. But for Arjun, she was something different. Completely friendly, playful, and even vulnerable at fleeting moments. Their relationship was defined not by traditional love, but by mutual respect and a shared knowledge of the games they performed in the shadows. They got to know each other well for a long time as Lynda was attempting to build her foothold in Phuket, understanding each other's darkest secrets and concerns. Arjun helped her in her early days. Since then, the two have built an unbreakable relationship.

It had been nearly a year since Lynda had descended upon the Nicobar with her entourage. Five women had accompanied her, each as striking as Lynda herself, a calculated move to shield her from prying eyes. "Distractions," she had called them, though Arjun knew that in her world, even beauty was a weapon.

He remembered her arrival vividly. The rhythmic hum of her private yacht's engine had announced her presence before the woman herself emerged on deck, her silhouette stark against the setting sun. Lynda had greeted him with a mischievous smile, her ice-blue eyes betraying nothing of the battles she fought in her life.

"What's the occasion, Lynda?" Arjun had asked when Arjun asked for her purpose to visit him few days back. Lynda had simply replied, "I wanted to see you, that's all."

"Do I need an occasion to see you, your birthday?" she added, her voice laced with amusement. Then, leaning closer, she whispered, "Perhaps I just missed you." watching as she slid her aviators onto her head.

They had spent the week at his villa, a whirlwind of indulgence that was overwhelming. By day, they lounged by the pool, sipping champagne and horse riding around the island. By night, they talked over candlelit dinners, their conversations cloaked with light humour and laughter but strictly no business discussions. They wanted a long-desired break from their work and dark life despite a few business-related calls that they had to take privately with each other's consent. Lynda was not just a passionate lover or a guest; she was an equal, someone who understood the delicate balance of power Arjun walked every day.

But even in their moments of intimacy, Arjun could sense the undercurrent of duality Lynda carried with her, on one side cutting-edge intelligence and ruthlessness and on the other side a soft and adorable mind behind the stunning beauty. Arjun was certain that before meeting him, Lynda would have to endure countless trials and men in this dark industry. She was the queen of subterranean lanes, but queens have enemies too and hers were not restricted to rivals in Phuket only. Rumours circulated that she was affiliated with the GRU and a member of the Red Sparrow squad, Russia's one of the most notorious women military intelligence squads, now part of FSB's Galmoradoun. Her expertise was honey trapping, where she used her unfathomable beauty to target political and business leaders. Part of her undercover operations included running a brothel franchise in Thailand. Arjun never inquired about her background or business, and she never did either. That was the unstated rule. They did not discuss their business with one another. There was no indication of curiosity.

The last night during her stay, as they sat on the beach under a canopy of stars, she had teased him about his growing empire in the Indian Ocean. "So, when do I get my cut of the spoils?" she asked, running her fingers through the sand.

Arjun had smirked, his gaze fixed on the horizon. "You get your cut when you stop bringing your spies to my island."

Lynda had laughed, a sound as smooth as silk. "You wound me, Arjun. They are not spies. They are just very curious women and my assistance to run my business, I brought them here for my own security and also to offer them a break."

It was a joke and the laughter had not lasted long. That night, Arjun had woken suddenly; he didn't also find her in his bed. When he turned to the different side, he found her standing on the balcony topless, staring at the sea, her expression uncharacteristically sombre. He went down from the bed and embraced her from the back, she only murmured absentmindedly.

"Do you ever think about walking away from all of these?" Her voice was barely audible over the crashing waves.

Arjun had been caught off guard but managed to say smirkingly, "And do what? Sell coconuts on the beach?"

She smiled faintly but did not respond. That was the last deep conversation they had before she left.

(Another two faces came into his mind—Shila and

their two-year-old son. Trust had become his greatest liability and the memory of them was a painful reminder of his brutal resolve. He had to see them burning alive at Haldia with their small roadside home located in a very poor neighbourhood beside the dock, a horrifying scene that still haunted him and sealed his fate. Many years later, despite that pain, he realized that event had eradicated his vulnerability in the true sense.

The thought of them, those he had once cherished, was a knife to his heart, but he steeled himself against the pain, focused intently on his work and built this dynasty, working like a monster after relocating to Andaman as a dock labourer long back after that blast. He realized that the normal life was not an option to live for him.

Since that day, Arjun knew he could not afford the luxury of having a family because of the vulnerability of him that came with his emotional attachments only. Relationships and love were perilous distractions in his line of work, where danger lurked at every corner and innocent lives were compromised. He had to make the ultimate choice—his own family—for his mission.

His family was caught in the crossfire of a brutal gang war, a tragedy that unfolded when he was a rising young leader within the perilous smuggling racket of Kalu Mastan's gang. The knowledge that his own mentor, who was harbouring personal animosities against his quick ascent, had planned their murder made the loss even more painful. Arjun's heart hardened with a cold, vengeful resolve. It was not those two lives only, that crossfire followed by the blast in that locality had taken several innocent lives because of his personal rivalry with his boss.

In an act of retribution, he confronted his mentor, dismantling the very trust and mentorship that had once guided him. The betrayal was met with a calculated and ruthless response; Arjun exacted his revenge by killing his mentor and disposing of the body in the most brutal way, feeding it to stray dogs on the road.

This act marked a point of no return, solidifying his commitment to his path and the sacrifices it demanded.

The experience left Arjun with a profound understanding of the cost of his chosen life. He steeled himself against the perils of attachment, knowing that his survival depended on his ability to remain detached and focused. The shadow of his past loomed large, driving him forward with an unyielding determination to succeed in a world where trust and relationships were luxuries he could no longer afford.

In those quiet, dark moments when their faces haunted him, he reaffirmed his commitment to his path. The price he paid was steep, but it was the only way to stay strong, to stay alive and to ensure his legacy in the shadowy underworld.)

MEETING FOR DEEP STATE
CHAPTER-11
@dibyenduchoudhury

Chapter 14: Meeting for Deep State

The neon-lit skyline of Dhaka shimmered under the night sky; a calm but deceptive storm was brewing within the corridors of power. Hidden deep in a colonial-style mansion in Gulshan, a group of shadowy figures gathered around a polished wooden table within the "Coffee House" private lounge. The room was dimly lit; its air was heavy with cigar smoke and the smell of freshly brewed coffee. The flicker of light danced across all the faces, casting long, ominous shadows. At the table's centre sat Zakir Khan of ISI, a suave intelligence operative known for his expertise in implementing "Deep State" strategies. He worked very closely with China's MSS and had been trained there. He was also operative when Syria's Al Bashar Government came into the picture and worked hand in hand with forming ISIS along with Iran and other forces. He doesn't look like a typical Pakistani; his deceptive European look might confuse people when he started speaking fluently in Bengali with his piercing blue eyes scanning the room. But his actions spoke louder than his appearance.

"Gentlemen, the stakes have never been higher. The current administration in Bangladesh is a thorn in the side of many interests regional as well as global. The biggest challenge is the economy is stable, the military is cooperative and their refusal to align fully with us and our plan...well, that's one of the problems we're here to solve. As we are aware, this current government is running in the support of RAW of India. Their intelligence created this country as their buffer zone, not only this country but also all of their neighbouring countries along with their borders. Every front we are fighting with them, but this time they can't win because of Mr. Thomas's support. He pointed to a man who was sitting in the middle of the table dressed in American business attire but of decent Chinese origin."

The room was filled with a diverse group of individuals from different countries, mainly comprised of diplomats, each one with their own vested interests, of course. However, the majority are the local Bangladeshi powerful businessmen with significant stakes in this region, political operatives skilled in the art of manipulation and former military personnel with the vindictive allegiances with the present government and earmarked hitmen of the previous government. The air was thick with the anticipation; each man present was aware of the high-risk, high-reward nature of their endeavor.

The plan was audacious: orchestrate a political shift in Bangladesh's government to instil a more pliable regime. The justification was very simple: allegations of corruption, civil unrest and human rights abuses. The tools? Proxy media campaigns designed to shape public opinion, financial incentives to sway key political figures and a network of local agitators ready to stir unrest when the time was right.

Zakir's voice was smooth, commanding attention as he outlined the strategy.

"We'll start by leveraging the media. Our proxy channels will report on government corruption and human rights abuses with the clear allegation of India's intelligence involvement and cooperation. We need to create a narrative that justifies our actions. Our targets would be the younger jobless generation, who are already angry with the constant joblessness. Simultaneously, we'll reach out to influential political figures of opposition as well as within the party—those with the power to tip the scales. Money talks, gentlemen; we have plenty of it."

One of the businessmen, a portly man with a cigar clamped between his teeth, nodded.

"I've got contacts in the media. We can start planting stories. What about the agitators?"

A figure at the far end of the table leaned forward, looking like a classical maulabi in his attire, revealing a scarred face and dead, cold voice with his calculating eyes.

"My men are trained and prepared. They had been waiting for this opportunity for years. We have been instructing locals to protest and create situations of public discontent. We only need the signal and the funds. The greatest time to wage it off is toward the end of this month, when one of the country's minority groups will hold a festival. However, several of our people are there, operating as a sleeper cell in India, surviving on forging official documents and illegally transporting people from here. I can extend my help to you on that extent if needed."

Zakir smiled, satisfied with the progress. "Excellent. We'll coordinate our efforts to ensure maximum impact. The protests will provide the justification for our intervention and our media channels will ensure the world sees it as a necessary political change with respect to age-old stagnancy and corruption."

As the meeting continued, the plan took on more detail. Timelines were set, tasks were assigned and contingencies were planned; money was transferred through hawala channels then and there. It was a meticulously crafted operation, one that required precision and coordination to succeed.

Outside the club in Gulshan, Dhaka, the vibrant pulse of the city continued unabated. The streets were bustling with activity—vendors shouting, neon lights flickering, and people moving in a ceaseless dance of life. But inside the dimly lit room, a different, far more sinister narrative was unfolding.

Within these walls, those who wanted to undermine India were rewriting the history of the tiny country. Their plan was cunning: to exploit Bangladesh's porous border with West Bengal, creating a covert route for smuggling and clandestine operations through Silhet to Assam and Tripura. These routes were crucial arteries in their strategy, connecting various points of their sinister network.

Meanwhile, Sinha was orchestrating chaos on another front, aiming to destabilize the southern part of India. The unrest in Manipur had already paved the way for greater infiltration, linking Myanmar, Bangladesh, and China in an extended web of the same conspiracy. The situation was precarious, with each move carefully calculated to weaken India's defenses and spread instability throughout the region.

As Zakir and his associates huddled over maps and documents, the weight of their mission was palpable.

They knew the stakes were incredibly high, but the potential rewards—control over a lucrative smuggling route, political leverage, and the disruption of a regional power—were worth the risk. Their eyes gleamed with ambition, greed and resolve, motivated by the thrill of defiance and the promise of power, which regrettably threatens a country's unity and the lives of its citizens.

Zakir, a mastermind of espionage and subterfuge, outlined their next steps with precision. "We need to ensure our contacts within the local authorities are activated," he told them with his voice low but resolute.

"Our success depends on their cooperation and the diversionary tactics we've planned. Our main goal is dividing India into different parts and cutting off the "Chicken Neck" to disconnect the Northeastern part from the mainland."

The room's atmosphere was thick with tension and anticipation. Every detail had been meticulously planned, from the bribery of officials to the logistics of moving illicit goods across borders. They had even identified key individuals within the Bangladeshi administrative framework who could be manipulated or coerced.

The clock was ticking, and each passing moment brought them closer to their goal. Zakir's associates, a mix of seasoned operatives and ambitious newcomers, nodded in agreement. They understood the gravity of their mission and the potential fallout if they failed. But failure was not an option they entertained.

The broader implications of their actions loomed large. A destabilized India would create a ripple effect, impacting the entire region's geopolitical stability. This was not just about immediate gains; it was about reshaping the balance of power in South Asia as part of China's expansionist approach.

As the meeting drew to a close, Zakir stood and looked out the window, his eyes scanning the bustling streets below. The world outside continued in its oblivious routine, unaware of the dark plans being hatched within that pristine club. He felt a surge of resolve, knowing that history would remember their actions. Last time this was their country which had been snatched by India and liberated.

"Our time is now," Zakir declared, turning back to face his comrades.

"We will execute our plan with precision and ensure that our efforts bear fruit. For too long, we have watched from the shadows. Now, we take control."

The conspirators dispersed, each to their respective roles, ready to set the wheels of their grand scheme in motion. The heart of the conspiracy beat with a relentless determination, poised to disrupt and redefine the future of an entire region. The intricate dance of deception and power had begun, and the outcome would shape the destiny of nations. The gathering dispersed, each man returning to his own sphere of influence, ready to set the plan in motion. Zakir lingered a moment longer, his thoughts already several steps ahead. He knew that regime changes were never simple; he failed here a couple of times, but with the right mix of pressure and persuasion, they were certainly possible. He remembered how they failed last time to hold the regime and this government took over. That's why he planned for the "Myth" this time along with his closest advisors for the collateral damage and mitigating the risk of failure. Intoxication was the key to unlocking the true potential where people lose their control over their minds. He knew that once people were under the influence, they would be more susceptible to manipulation and less likely to resist the new regime.

The neon lights of Dhaka flickered at night because of low voltage as Zakir stepped out into the night, the cool air a stark contrast to the charged atmosphere of the club. The city looked like a chessboard and he was ready to make his moves. The game was on and he was confident in their strategy. He already received a text from Sinha from Colombo to initiate "Project Eclipse" last night.

Stepping out into the bustling streets of Dhaka, Zakir's sharp eyes scanned the throngs of people and the cacophony of daily life. He spotted Rasheed, his trusted auto driver, waiting patiently in his three-wheeled auto-rickshaw. In Bangladesh, where these autos weaved through traffic with an agility that cars couldn't match, Rasheed was the perfect driver for his quick and discreet transport.

As Zakir approached, Rasheed flashed him a knowing glance, starting the engine with a practiced hand. The auto-rickshaw buzzed to life, and Zakir slipped into the back seat, feeling the familiar hum beneath him. The small vehicle darted into the traffic, navigating the labyrinthine streets with ease. They sped towards Savar, a suburban hideout far from the prying eyes of Dhaka's crowded urban centre. The journey through the bustling cityscape gave Zakir a moment to reflect on the night's events. He was aware that his plans could reshape the geopolitical landscape and the weight of such responsibility was as thrilling as it was terrifying too.

 Rasheed maneuverer the auto with finesse, cutting through narrow alleyways and bypassing traffic snarls that would have stalled a car. The swift, bumpy ride was a reminder of the agility and resourcefulness required in their line of work. The hum of urban life gradually replaced the noise as they left the city behind.

Arriving at the secluded hideout in Savar, Zakir stepped out of the auto-rickshaw, taking a moment to steady himself. The air was different here—calmer, yet heavy with anticipation. Rasheed, ever vigilant, kept watch as Zakir entered the hideout. The small, nondescript building belied the importance of the activities within. Inside, a network of operatives was working tirelessly, collating information, planning operations, and communicating with contacts across borders.

Zakir was sure, Victor Lang had every intention of wielding that power to reshape the landscape of this region.

THE DIGITAL
SIEGE
Chapter-16
@dibyenduchoudhury

Chapter 16: The Digital Siege

In Dhaka's enormous market areas and bazaars, voices of discontent began to grow louder soon. Social media platforms started erupting with charges of government ineptitude and rumours of secret deals with foreign powers along with the proximity with foreign intelligence. Carefully prepared films of protests, some were off course staged and real, but the majority were produced with the help of deepfake with swamped timelines. The story was very simple but effective: the government had lost touch with the common people and was abusing its position in power for a long time, needing a change because of several governance failures, specially creating jobs for the youth within the country. The narrative was that the military and power brokers had hijacked democracy, leaving the country in the hands of people who intended to misuse their positions and authority. In such a situation, none of the inhabitants felt comfortable or secure; additionally, everyone gradually joined the bandwagon for the sake of change; no one questioned the essential questions about the ramifications of their actions.

Behind these attempts was a sophisticated network of agents operating from a secure site on the outskirts of the city where Zakir lived in Basar. His vast server room pumped out content round the clock, while teams of analysts tracked the nation's pulse via TRP ratings and social media engagement. Hired local influencers, journalists, and opposition leaders were carefully co-opted, with their platforms and started propagating the message of discontent. Zakir's cover was a digital marketing trainer, so he assembled a group of educated and effective local students who knew the pulse of the youth. He originally recruited students looking for additional money but then expanded his crew and made the enterprise full-time before unleashing the national drama of lies and deceit.

Only a few people knew about that facility, which looked like a fortress of technology and secrecy. Rows of servers pulsed with activity, their blinking lights creating an eerie glow in the dimly lit area. Analysts sat at their workstations, their eyes fixed on displays displaying real-time data along with the feed from social media, news outlets, and encrypted chats. Every piece of information, every trend, was examined to ensure the narrative remained consistent and engaging with real-time analytics shown on a dashboard on the main LED screen in the middle of the wall visible to all.

The operators operated with military precision because of their training and enthusiasm for the first paid live assignment, designed communications that tapped the public's mounting discontent. They took every chance to heighten the sense of despair and dissatisfaction. Carefully timed leaks and spectacular headlines kept the public on edge, calling into question the legitimacy of their leaders. The goal was to incite revolution and overthrow the government.

In the middle of this digital assault, a group of professional hackers in Abbottabad, Pakistan, began working tirelessly to enter government databases and collect critical information. Pakistani hackers affiliated with Inter-Services Intelligence (ISI) worked as part of Pakistan's larger cyber-espionage operations. These entities were accused of engaging in cyber warfare with the goal of destabilizing opponents, gathering intelligence, and spreading misinformation. The hackers were known to target government bodies, military organizations, and key infrastructure in several countries. The gang nicknamed 'Silent Libra' of Advanced Persistent Threat (APT36) was particularly adept at utilizing social engineering tactics to gain access to sensitive information. They deployed tools like Crimson RAT

(Remote Access Trojan) to gain access to sensitive networks. Their purpose was to craft stories based upon corruption and misconduct, further undermining public trust in the government. Each successful, deliberated, and crafted breach was quietly celebrated, with the data carefully evaluated and spread via multiple routes through encrypted data scrambling technology.

The masterminds behind this operation were aware of the importance of building public perception and opinion based upon crafted media. They understood controlling the narrative was critical to destabilizing the government; during the information era, therefore, the propaganda was employed as an instrument for war. They slowly succeeded in planting seeds of doubt and mistrust, resulting in a wave of dissent that would be difficult to overcome.

As the days turned into weeks, the results of their labour became more apparent. Due to the constant stream of incendiary content, protests broke out all over the city and across the nation. The streets of Dhaka, once bustling with daily life and commercial activities, started reverberating with the chants of protesters seeking change.

Zakir, the mastermind behind the operation, moved through the facility with a sense of purpose. His sharp eyes missed almost nothing and his mind was always several steps ahead. He knew that controlling the narrative was key to their success. The government's image had to be tarnished beyond repair and the seeds of doubt had to be sown deep within the populace. The best bait to dismantle the friendship and trust among the clans, races and religions to initiate the civil war. He knew some people would dies as part of collateral damage but at the end the power would be snatched by his supportive friends in Government.

"Keep the pressure on," Zakir instructed one of his lead analysts. "We need more stories about corruption and inefficiency. Highlight the protests, make them look larger than life. And ensure our influencers are pushing the message hard. I need hourly analytics on my table."

The intensity of the commotion caught the government off guard, and it attempted to regain control. Zakir, however, realized that this was a double-edged sword and that any mistake the government made, such as firing shots and spilling blood to contain the mob, may result in civil war. Their attempts to refute the narrative were met with scepticism and scorn. The operators' scheme ultimately worked and the country's stability started shaking.

The students were relieved because of the local disturbances; "Silent Libra's" analysts took it off and continued to work from their secured facility, never looking away from their screens by taking the control of Zakir's server on remote access, so that Bangladeshi intelligence agency never could trace back their digital footprints. They understood that the struggle for control was far from done. Every click, share, and comment served as data points in their continuous fight to influence Bangladesh's future. Zakir alone started observing the entire movement in their dashboard entire day in the vacant facility.

Students studying digital marketing who started the game as part of their full-time jobs as analysts before the country's upheaval and breakout were utterly unaware that their ignorance and naivete had ultimately cost them dearly because they were sitting idle during the unrest totally unaware that they had only started the fire somewhere that would eventually catch fire and burn them down as well. Their innocence and requirements had been capitalized and captured by Zakir to destabilize their own country only.

Meanwhile, in the heart of Dhaka, the results of their work were starting to appear. Protests sprang out in major sites, attracting hundreds of disillusioned individuals. Some were genuine, motivated by legitimate complaints, while others were staged by

Zakir's network. The distinction between fact and fiction eroded, resulting in a combustible mixture that threatened to boil over at any time.

Local news stations began covering the stories, increasing the atmosphere of discontent. Journalists, some naively and others complicit, covered the mounting anger with vigour. The government's attempts to contradict the narrative were viewed with scepticism, as their words were drowned out by the never-ending stream of negative ads.

In the vacant facility, Zakir started watching the events started unfolding with satisfaction as per their desire. The idea began to work when he discovered that bogus videos pumped by his team from Pakistan were becoming viral and being distributed in loops print and digital media. The administration was on the defensive mode, attempting to keep control of public disruption. But he knew it was just the beginning. The true challenge was in maintaining the momentum and pushing the situation to a tipping point to breach the system.

"Activate our next phase," Zakir instructed someone through a popular App works on encrypted technology on voice as well as data. "We must raise the protests. Use our contacts to encourage additional demonstrations across. And start disclosing details about alleged ties with foreign powers now with forged documents. We need to make the government appear to be selling out the country."

The squad jumped into action, their efforts multiplied. Messages were exchanged, calls were placed, and the gears of manipulation turned increasingly faster. The protests intensified, and Dhaka's streets became a battleground for ideologies and agendas.

The city which used to get busy some weeks back in the morning started looking like a battle ground in few weeks with incandescent protesters, mobs were fighting with police, some tires were burning on the roads with several stores looted and burnt. Protesters battled with police and their chants echoed throughout the tiny streets. Fires raged in the distance, casting a terrible glare over the scene. The air was thick with anxiety, with the aroma of smoke and tear gas blending in a heady mixture.

Zakir drove around the streets at nights in various areas with Rasheed despite the curfews, overlooking the pandemonium below. He felt a rush of excitement, the force of his obvious influence. This was his domain, a world where information was the most powerful weapon and those damages were the sign of his victory drawn out of sadistic pleasure.

The night drew on, and Dhaka remained in tumult. The whispers of discontent had turned into a roar sooner and Zakir watched it all with determination, preparing to steer the storm he had unleashed to its inevitable conclusion. The battle for control was only a matter of time he knew.

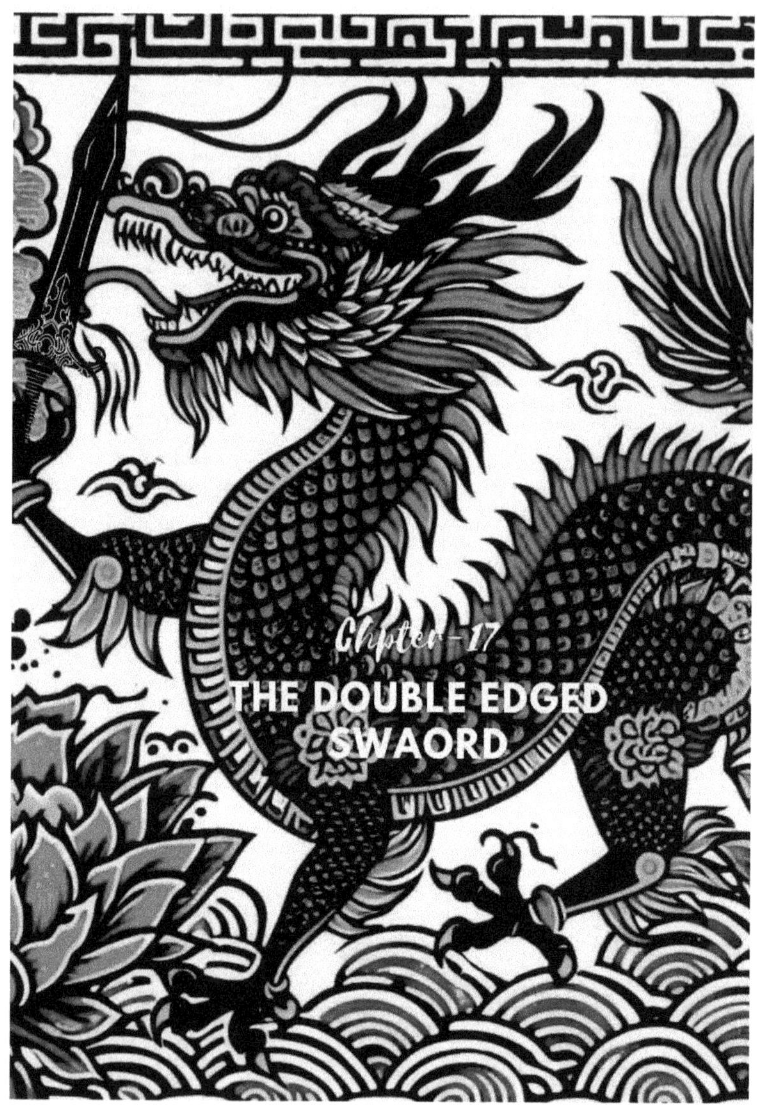
Chapter - 17
THE DOUBLE EDGED
SWAORD

Chapter 17: The Double-edged Sword

Meanwhile, Zakir's agents were carrying out a careful strategy to infiltrate and damage the ruling party itself. They meticulously selected their targets and made promises and offers of lucrative contracts, retirement funds, new positions, new governments, and political refuge to disillusioned insiders. The goal was to cause a schism at the very top, pitting comrades against one another and spreading division among the ranks. As tensions within the ruling party grew, Zakir's operatives worked behind the scenes to exploit any fissures that appeared. Slowly but steadily, the once-unified front began to splinter, with high-ranking members trading suspicions and accusations. The strategy was going wonderfully, with Zakir's ultimate goal of undermining the ruling party in sight. Their carefully planned strategy would eventually bear fruit.

Zakir tested the waters with Sinha, sending a cryptic message: "The time is ripe. Send The Scorpion to bite" from Gwadar. Zakir was acutely aware that "Myth" had the potential to further destabilize the government. This shipment, planned to be sent to India, had been strategically lying at the Gwadar port for last few months, awaiting the perfect moment to land in Bangladesh.

In a dimly lit room, Zakir convened with one of his key operatives, a man known only as "The Broker." The room, filled with the hum of computers at the backdrop and the glow of LED screen with the dashboard showing all the parameters of analytics caught skyrocketed, was his nerve centre of that clandestine operation at Basar. Zakir leaned forward, his eyes piercing and intense.

"How are our efforts progressing?" The Broker smirked, exuding confidence.

"We've got a few high-ranking officials on the hook. They're desperate for a way out of this country to US, and our offers are too tempting to refuse." Zakir nodded, satisfied with the progress.

"Good. Keep the pressures on. We need them to start turning on each other. The more chaos, the much better."

The Broker outlined the latest developments, detailing how they had infiltrated various echelons of the ruling party by name. Discreet meetings were held in secluded locations, where promises of wealth and safety were whispered to the disenchanted. The seeds of betrayal were being sown, and the fractures within the party were beginning to show. He gave the lists of accounts and disbursal amounts written by the side of the names.

The ship named "The Scorpion," was prepped and ready, its cargo a ticking time bomb designed to destabilize the nation and make the future of the country crippled. It had entered Bangladesh through Chittagong Port from Gwadar Port, Pakistan and docked just as the protests escalated beyond Dhaka, spreading like wildfire across the country.

The plan was meticulously crafted to synchronize the release of the shipment with the peak of political turmoil, ensuring the maximum impact on youth. As the unrest grew, the operatives knew that the timing had to be perfect. The cargo on "The Scorpion" was not just a physical threat but a venomous chaos they intended to unleash. The ship "The Scorpion" lay in wait, its cargo ready to be unleashed at the perfect moment. The operatives knew that their actions would have far-reaching consequences and they were determined to tip the scales in their favour.

The operators moved precisely, planning every aspect to coincide with the rising protests. They expected the instability to have the greatest impact on the youth, who were already dissatisfied and angry. By focusing on this group, they sought to create a difficult-to-control movement, increasing the availability of "Myth" in their possession. Their mission's success is dependent on their ability to capitalize on political instability on one side while directing Myth supplies on the other to intensify discontent in their favour. The inebriated mob was their most powerful weapon, causing mayhem and devastation before eventually overturning the government. No technologies could detect or quantify the level of drunkenness in "Myth".

Back in the large vacant office space of Zakir and The Broker read over detailed maps and dossiers outlining the supply chain and contact information. Their principal distribution outlets were the madrasas of their supporters and relatives.

"Our contacts in the military are also showing signs of wavering loyalty," The Broker stated. "If we can turn them, it will be a significant blow to the government's stability."

Zakir's eyes glowed with the excitement of a chess master preparing the board for checkmate. "Excellent. Make certain to emphasize the perception that their interests are compatible with ours. Fear and opportunity are strong motivators.

The broker nodded, recognizing the subtle art of manipulation.

"We've also launched a misinformation campaign to muddy the waters. False leads, doctored documents—anything to keep the cops guessing."

Zakir leaned back, a rare smile spreading over his lips. "We're on the verge of something monumental. Our efforts are like a coiled spring, ready to unleash disaster at any time. The government will never know what hit them in reality."

The stakes were extremely high, as were the possible benefits for Zakir. He was creating a magnificent symphony of deception and force, with each note meticulously prepared to reverberate with maximum effect. Zakir had already received an invitation from his nation to come back and serve as ISI's second lieutenant to plan the game for Myanmar last night. The best part was Zakir knew the head of ISI was unknown to everyone, and he had heard that he was so passionate that he exclusively worked in sensitive domains. His name was Ishtiaq Khan, but no one had actually seen him.

The meeting ended, but the operation continued with relentless intensity. Zakir knew that every move they made brought them closer to their goal. The fabric of power in Bangladesh was being rewritten, and he was the unseen hand guiding the pen. He was also happy to receive the promotion. He was finally being recognized for his hard work and dedication.

As Zakir and his operatives moved forward, the political landscape shifted beneath them. The game was afoot, and the destiny of nations hung in the balance. The thrill of the hunt drove them on, each step calculated, each action precise. The true test of their cunning and resolve was about to begin.

Zakir knew the best time to launch the "Myth". One night while returning from a meeting, Rasheed asked him "Sir, you are looking happy, have you got your promotion at work because of your work?"

"Yes, how do you know?" Zakir replied with a sly smile, "But how do you know?"

"Nothing, I just heard it through the grapevine." Rasheed told.

"This cannot be known to anyone outside. I don't know how you found out." Zakir told him in a soft tone, but he remained intrigued because Rasheed had been his auto driver since the first day of his arrival in Bangladesh and he spoke very little and had little interest in learning anything about him.

Rasheed added in a quiet voice, "Let me know when you want to proceed with your travel plans," which astounded Zakir.

Who was Rasheed? How did he know all of the latest news? Who was he associated to at ISI?

There were so many questions, yet he refrained from asking any more. He was certain he was not a simple auto driver, and Rasheed's background needed to be examined before approaching him with information.

SHIF·EE HOUSE
CHAPTER-18
THE INTELLIGENCE
COUP

Chapter 18: The Intelligence Coup

The Bangladesh intelligence agency, famous with the name Directorate of National Security (DNS), however, was not blind while the entire crisis was unfolding. Brigadier Tariq Rahman from Military Intelligence headed the department; a sharp and no-nonsense officer, he had been tracking the unusual uptick in anti-government sentiment with unwavering attention. During a midnight briefing with his team, he laid out his findings with precision.

"This isn't organic," Tariq told, his voice cutting through the room like a knife. "Someone's pulling the strings. And I intend to find out who."

His team, a group of seasoned analysts and field agents, listened intently. Tariq's reputation for being thorough and relentless was well-known, and his words carried weight. Each member of the team understood the gravity of their task.

One of the analysts, a young woman named Ayesha, spoke up, her voice steady.

"Sir, we've traced several large transfers to NGOs and media outlets. The funds are coming from offshore accounts, but the trail is faint."

Tariq's eyes narrowed. "Faint isn't good enough. I want concrete evidence. Keep digging."

Ayesha nodded, determination in her eyes. "Yes, sir."

The team worked tirelessly, piecing together the puzzle. They began to uncover connections to shell companies in Singapore, Dubai, and London. The fingerprints were faint but undeniable: a concerted effort to destabilize the government and the funding was evident. Late one night, Tariq called a meeting with his top officials. The room was filled with tension as they reviewed the latest findings. Charts and graphs illuminated with fluorescent light, a very well-lit space, casting no shadows on the walls.

"Look at this," Tariq said, pointing to a map dotted with red marks. "Each transfer and shell company leads back to a common nexus. We're dealing with a highly coordinated operation."

His top officers, seasoned in the art of counterintelligence, exchanged knowing glances.

They had seen such patterns before but never on this scale.

Ayesha, who had been instrumental in unearthing the connections, presented the latest intelligence.

"We've identified a key operative coordinating the funds from Hong Kong. His name is Victor Lang, a known financier with ties to various extremist groups and MSS."

Tariq's jaw tightened. "Victor Lang. I should have known. He's been on our radar for years. We need to move faster before he covers his tracks. Share the intel with our international allies to alert them."

In the heart of the intelligence agency, the lights burned brightly as Tariq and his team prepared for the decisive move. The battle lines were drawn, and the fate of the nation rested on their shoulders. The shadowy figures behind the destabilization efforts would soon face the full force of Bangladeshi intelligence, as Tariq Rahman led the charge against the unseen enemy.

"We've identified several key players," Tariq began. "These shell companies are funnelling money to our NGOs and media. They're trying to buy influence and create chaos."

One of his officers, Captain Rahim, leaned forward. "What's our next move, Sir?"

Tariq's gaze was steely. "We need to cut off their funding to choke down their machinery and expose their operatives on the ground. Start with the NGOs. If we can disrupt their cash flow, we can slow them down."

Rahim nodded. "Understood, we will freeze all of their bank accounts everywhere. We'll also need to keep an eye on the media. They're being used to spread disinformation and initiated the propaganda."

Tariq agreed. "Exactly. We need to control the narrative. If we can prove that these stories are being planted, we can start to turn public opinion back in our favour." The game of cat and mouse had begun, it was only a matter of time who moved smarter than whom.

Ayesha told in an aggrieved voice," Sir, I doubt we don't have that much time, because they planned and initiated their information warfare at least much ahead than us. We've traced it now and changing the narratives would take some time. Already they've leaked several confidential documents to the public. This is a well-planned move and they're well ahead."

Rahim said, " We traced a server and all the digital footprints are taking us there, the IP is US based but

I feel like it's a decoy behind a proxy server. We need some time to encrypt the real location, I'm sure its somewhere in Bangladesh only."

Meanwhile, "Myth" had already been released, targeting youth to further destabilize the country, as Zakir's masterstroke. Access to "Myth" caused mayhem in Bangladesh.

Tariq recognized they didn't have much time; the counter-strike approach would be to protect the president straight away, before any damage could be done to him.

He was wondering how these folks were able to infiltrate so simply. Foreign countries are definitely involved because of the funding nature; however, the question still remained even such funding could have also happened if the opposition found a funding agency for their own benefit and begin the internal cue. The sources of finance remained mysterious. Tariq realized they had to act quickly before the situation worsened and catch hold of few NGO's and Media houses head for further enquiry.

He issued an order: "Okay, identify the top-funded people and get their last ten days of phone conversations and photographs; tap their phone and initiate further investigation by tonight." We need a hint. I need to speak with the president and return in a few hours. I want to hear those tapes for myself before drawing any conclusions." and left the room.

Chapter-18
The Boiling Point
@DibyenduChoudhury

Chapter 18: The Boiling Point

As protests intensified suddenly and gone out of the hands within few days, so did the pressure on the administration. Clashes between police and demonstrators became common, the streets of Dhaka echoing with chants for change, people started behaving like mads. The ruling party, under siege, began to fracture. Cabinet ministers resigned and factions emerged, each vying for control or looking for allies to encash the opportune moment. There had been a saying that power corrupts and absolute power corrupts absolutely.

Zakir watched the turmoil unfold from his safe haven when the market was slammed by the "Myth". He leaned back in his chair, a contented smile spreading across his lips. "We're almost there; operation accomplished and time to move out now." His voice was raspy." to himself, "One more push and they'll implode."

"What was that? That's the effect of the release of Myth, it just exploded everything. What is that?"

Tariq inquired of his team. The team looked at each other nervously, unsure of how to answer.

"The chemical name is methamphetamine; the new synthetic narcotic known as "Myth," has emerged as a formidable force in the global drug trade recently. Unlike classical narcotics like heroin or cocaine, methamphetamine is alarmingly easy to produce and ship undetected and these people released it via Chittagong port seven days back through a shipment." Ayesha reported and continued "The police are investigating the matter."

"The drug reached to the students and then the entire chanting and disruption to the country gone beyond anyone's control. We're only left out with the option of bringing Army and firing on innocent and intoxicated people. The peace will come now at the cost of blood only." Rahim said.

"It is the failure of RAB, but it too late to get into the blame game." Ayesha added.

Rahim stated, "A modest 100 square feet is all that is required to make this strong drug, making it a favourite among clandestine chemists. The market value of methamphetamine is astonishing; 100 MTon is worth almost Rs 70,000 crore in New York City alone. Its demand in the United States is quite high, resulting in a lucrative but dangerous trade. The market for methamphetamine in India, Bangladesh, and other South Asian nations is still in its early stages, but it is the most affordable and convenient option for all users, offering the same sensations with increased sexual desire. Furthermore, our chemists are claiming that because it is synthetic, persons who become addicted find it difficult to quit."

Meanwhile, the Prime Minister of Bangladesh, a man once revered for his leadership, found himself isolated and totally vulnerable. The walls of his palace, once a symbol of power, now felt like a prison. The protests outside grew louder and the calls for his resignation became deafening.

In a war room within the palace, the Prime Minister met with his closest advisors and allies. The tension was palpable outside and the air was thick with fear and uncertainty.

"We can't hold out much longer," one advisor said, his voice trembling. "The people are turning mad against us. We need to act. We can deploy the military to control this maddening mob."

The Prime Minister's face was etched with worry; apparently, he was also disheartened.

"Deploying the military means more killing, more destruction, which I don't want. If they want a better leader than me, they have every right. Why shall I kill them and suppress their likings and disliking by force? I shall surrender, but I won't abandon my country."

Another advisor, a seasoned diplomat, leaned forward.

"There's another option. We've been in touch with other intelligence operatives who are our allies. They can help you seek political asylum; we already have different options. It's the only way to ensure your safety and regroup for a counterstrategy."

The President's eyes widened. "Political Asylum? Leaving my country in the hands of these traitors?"

The diplomat nodded solemnly. "It's a temporary measure, Sir. We need to survive to fight another day. This mob will kidnap and hang you if you stay here. We can't afford to lose you."

Brigadier Tariq Rahman stood before the Prime Minister; his voice subdued but urgent.

"Sir, this entire situation has been orchestrated by our adversaries and it has been exacerbated by a dangerous narcotic known as 'Myth. You may be seeing these mobs demanding your resignation, but everything been framed against your government; our team collected enough proof. The situation has spiralled out of control, and we don't have much time to contain it. This is not the time for disheartening; we also don't have much time for the risk management and arrest this unrest."

The Prime Minister's face was etched with concern as he listened.

Tariq continued, "Before we could act, they reached the youth, who have now become the epicentre of this chaos. The people you see demanding your resignation are not in their normal state. They are chemically intoxicated and high on euphoria. The damage is beyond our immediate control."

Tariq paused, the weight of his words hanging in the air and all the people in that room were listening to him carefully.

"We must act swiftly, but the reality is grim. The best we can hope for is to stabilize the situation and prevent further escalation. Tomorrow may bring a better day, but only if you remain safe and alive."

The Prime Minister nodded, understanding the gravity of the situation.

"What do you propose, Brigadier?"

Tariq's eyes hardened with resolve.

"We need to isolate the sources of 'Myth' and cut off their supply lines once you evacuate this country. Simultaneously, we must launch a counter-narrative to regain control of the public's perception. It's a multi-front battle, but we have no other choice and this needs time."

The Prime Minister took a deep breath, his mind racing with the implications.

"Do whatever it takes, Brigadier. Our nation's future depends on it."

Reluctantly, the Prime Minister agreed. The plan was set in motion. Under the cover of night, allied intelligence operatives infiltrated the palace. Disguised as palace staff, they moved with precision; their mission was very much clear: extract the Prime Minister and his family through a safe passage, out of the country with his very close aides for better tomorrow."

In the dead of night, the Prime Minister and his family members, flanked by his loyal advisors and the allied intelligence operatives, made their way through the palace's hidden passages in different convoys. The sounds of faraway protests resonated through the black night. The Prime Minister was aware that the judgments made that night would determine the fate of the nation.

As they approached the palace's basement garage, a fleet of unmarked vehicles waited for them. The Prime Minister paused, glancing back at the palace one last time.

"I will return," he said, his voice full of conviction.

The caravan rushed through Dhaka's shadowy streets, skirting important routes and checkpoints as it headed to the military airbase to exit the nation. The voyage was tense, with each instant carrying the possibility of detection.

They finally arrived on the outskirts of the city, where an unmarked private plane awaited them in the military hangar. The Prime Minister boarded the plane with his family, his heart burdened from his decision. As the plane lifted off, he stared out the window, watching his beloved city vanish into the distance below.

The war for Bangladesh has begun a new chapter. The Prime Minister, now a fugitive, was resolved to fight for his country's destiny. As the plane flew over the night sky, the Prime Minister realized that the journey ahead would be long and difficult. But he was prepared. The war for his country's soul had just recently begun.

But the doubts persisted: "Who and how could individuals betray him, despite his family's unwavering loyalty to this country? Can individuals be this unworthy and disloyal?"

Only the words in his father's final letter kept him going.

MV ORION
CAPTURED
Chapter-19

Chapter 19: MV Orion Captured

The Indian Coast Guard's INS Vikramaditya surged through the dark on the turbulent waters of the Bay of Bengal, its radar systems scanning the horizon with unwavering precision. Commander Aarav Thakur stood on the bridge, his sharp eyes fixed on the monitors. The tension was palpable; an untraceable Starlink satellite phone signal had been detected hours ago near the Indian international maritime border. The signal's sudden appearance and its irregular transmissions suggested something mysterious was happening in the region.

The chatter in the operations room crackled with urgency.

"Commander, we've intercepted an anomaly," reported Lieutenant Meera Iyer, her voice steady but strained.

"A cargo ship, MV Orion, is displaying erratic movements. It is deviating from its declared route to Port Blair. AIS transponders are off and it is heading dangerously close to the Indian mainland."

"Scramble the boarding team," Aarav ordered, his tone decisive. "And notify Chennai HQ. This could be our lead."

"There is a decoy they use for deceptive purposes. Therefore, be vigilant for both the signals and run parallel." Shivansh told Aarav over the phone.

As the Vikramaditya closed in on the target, the skies began to darken. The Bay of Bengal churned with waves as a storm brewed on the horizon, adding another layer of peril to the unfolding mission.

Meanwhile, miles away, a small fishing trawler bobbed uneasily in the water. Onboard, six women from Myanmar were working silently and were looking distressed, their eyes darting nervously as the wind picked up. Beneath the deck, in a hollowed-out chamber, hundreds of kilograms of Myth were carefully packed and waiting for transfer in a vacuum fish container.

Their role was clear: to create a diversion. By traveling into Indian seas, they would divert attention away from the MV Orion, allowing the fishing trawler to pass undetected. However, their scheme failed due to the use of the Starlink satellite phone to access the internet.

One of the women, Ma Thiri, whispered to her friend, "The signal is weak." We shouldn't have used our phone to access the internet."

San Aye, the other woman, wore a sad expression. "We do not have a choice; waiting here without further instruction can also make us stranded for hours and getting captured."

The sudden roar of engines cut off their whispered conversation. A smaller interceptor vessel from the Vikramaditya appeared on the horizon, slicing through the waves.

Back in Vikramaditya, Aarav received the report. "The fishing trawler is within our borders, sir. There are six people on board, all of them are women and most likely unarmed.

"Intercept and board," Aarav ordered. "But don't lose sight of Orion. That is our main aim."

The boarding team landed quickly on the trawler, armed and ready. The women surrendered without resistance, their expressions a mix of fear and anger. As the officers investigated the vessel, the concealed compartments were discovered, revealing the wealth of narcotics.

A message crackled over Aarav's comms. "Commander, the MV Orion is within our vicinity, not responding to our signal."

The MV Orion loomed ahead, a massive shadow against the darkening sky; it might be changing its course. Aarav's voice was calm but firm as he addressed the crew.

"This is where it counts, team. That ship cannot reach Indian shores, I doubt suddenly it might change its course and get in Sri Lankan border. Deploy the RHIBs and prepare for an aggressive boarding."

As the Coast Guard's small, fast boats sped toward the cargo ship, the storm intensified. Lightning forked across the sky, illuminating the scene in brief, electric flashes. The Orion's crew spotted the approaching vessels and panicked, increasing speed and veering erratically.

"Starboard engine is faltering," Meera reported from the operations room. "They won't outrun us in this weather."

Aarav seized the moment. "Bring us alongside. Boarding team, move in!"

Under cover of the storm, the Coast Guard officers jumped onto the deck of the Orion. The crew attempted to resist with rudimentary weapons, causing chaos to erupt. Aarav led the charge, using his tactical skills to disarm and overpower the ship's captain.

The team located the cargo hold below deck. It was stacked with cartons labelled as medical supplies, but a cursory examination revealed they were actually sealed waterproof packing.

Shivansh was correct; this was the deception.

Meera's voice came through the communications system. "Sir, this is it." That boat was the actual package we had been tracking. We have the largest deployment of narcotics in tons aboard the boat with the fish tin cans and six women, estimated to be worth $10 billion. This is the largest seizure so far of "myth" in India."

Aarav breathed sharply, a combination of relief and stern determination. "Secure both the ship and the boat. "We're taking both to Chennai Port."

As the Vikramaditya towed the captured Orion as well as the fishing boat back to Indian shores, the storm finally began to abate. Aarav stood on the deck, the wind whipping through his hair, contemplating the magnitude of what they had uncovered. The conspiracy was larger than they had imagined, with tendrils stretching from Myanmar to the Andaman Islands and from there into South India either through Chennai or Kerala. The capture of the Orion was a victory, but it was only one battle in a larger war against the insidious network determined to destabilize India.

The Bay of Bengal was calm once more, but Aarav, Meera, Shivansh and Riya knew it was only the eye of the storm. Shivansh reports back to Delhi to Kavitha Nair to inform her of the good news. Kavitha Nair Madam called and congratulated the Gelisko team.

Aarav turned to Meera. "This was a good day for, but the war is yet to begin. They are desperate enough to use Starlink and send decoys; imagine their ruthlessness; they are definitely already planning their next move. Let us make sure we are ready when they do next."

Shivansh gave a proud look at him. The entire team flew on the urgent call through the Indian Navy's helicopter that night for the next day's meeting in Delhi.

Chapter 20

THE SHADOW
CONFLICT LOOMS

@DibyenduChoudhury

Chapter 20: The Shadow Conflict looms.

The tension was tangible, in the war room of Kavitha Iyer. Shivansh, Riya, Aarav and Meera sat around the conference table, their faces illuminated by the glow of the monitors displaying maps and intelligence reports. On a secure video call from Russia, the Honourable Prime Minister was connected and his expression was stern, as he waited for the latest developments as he was aware of the operation but was flying, therefore unaware about the seizure and volume.

Kavitha stood at the head of the table, ready to deliver her report. She took a deep breath and began, "Good morning, Prime Minister Sir, ladies and gentlemen connected in this meeting virtually. We have urgent news regarding the Arakan Army in Rakhine State, Myanmar. The situation is escalating rapidly, signalling the same as Bangladesh."

She clicked a button and a detailed map of Rakhine State appeared on the main screen. "Nestled along the rugged coastline of Myanmar, Rakhine State has long been a theatre of conflict and political intrigue. The Arakan Army, a potent insurgent group started in 2009 by the members of the ethnic Rakhine community, is at the centre of this unrest. Their mission: to secure greater autonomy for their homeland and wrest control from the grip of the Myanmar military force."

She added, "Since the military takeover in 2021, the AA's power has increased enormously. They now control over 80% of Rakhine State, including critical locations such as the state capital, Sittwe, and the economically vital Kyaukpyu Special Economic Zone (SEZ), which also houses the port. The AA now has complete authority over two Chinese projects and partial control over eight others in the region, for a total of ten projects under its sway. Among these, the Kyaukpyu deep-sea port and SEZ are particularly important. The AA's presence in Ramree Township, which is close to Kyaukpyu, suggests that the organization may have a role in how Chinese development proceeds within the SEZ. "The Scorpion" loaded "Myth" over there, and subsequently the fish trawler arrived from that port. Our intelligence showed that "The Scorpion" planned to enter Chennai first, then Kerala, and finally Gwadar. Later, the same container was delivered to Chittagong port and securely returned to its original location."

The Prime Minister squinted his eyes as he listened closely. Kavitha advanced to the next slide, which displayed photographs of recent confrontations. "The crisis in Rakhine State has developed into a deadly war, with high-intensity battles between the AA and the Myanmar military becoming commonplace. The civilian population has suffered greatly, with thousands displaced from homes, particularly Rohingya and ethnic Rakhine. The humanitarian situation that has emerged will allow illegal migration, arms smuggling, and other criminal businesses to grow throughout Southeast Asia via various routes and methods.

Aarav interjected, "With your permission, Madam, can the AA govern effectively under these conditions? Do they have the capacity to address the socio-economic needs of Rakhine's residents while fending off military assaults?"

Kavitha shook her head. "That remains uncertain. The AA's governance strategy and their ability to maintain stability in the region will be crucial in the months and years to come and need to be observed."

She then introduced a more sinister element. "Here is where the plot thickens. Entering to the deep state theory—intelligence suggesting that hidden, powerful forces within the government or military are manipulating events for their own shadowy interests. Analysts over here believe that these covert actors are subtly influencing the AA's rise and the ongoing conflict in Myanmar's complex political environment in an effort to destabilize the area for particular political purposes."

Shivansh leaned forward; his interest piqued. "So, we're dealing with a much larger conspiracy than just the AA?"

"Exactly," Kavitha confirmed. "Internationally, the situation in Rakhine State has not gone unnoticed. Neighbouring countries and global powers are closely monitoring these developments, wary of the implications for regional stability. Taking lessons from Bangladesh. The AA's potential connections with external actors, whether for support or strategic alliances. These layers of complexity add to an already intricate scenario."

Riya, who had been quietly taking notes, spoke up. Deep state theory suggests a grander design beyond Rakhine's borders, requiring us to navigate deceit, power plays, and clandestine operations while addressing real threats."

As the conversation progressed, Kavitha announced, "Given the recent success of the Myth seizure and our coordinated efforts with other departments, I am pleased to inform you all that you have been ordered to join a special task force with the Hon'ble Prime Minister's intervention and permission, the orders are already posted to your higher-ups for immediate effect. You all will be now working in tandem with NSA's Raghav and RAW's Tuhina."

Raghav, a seasoned National Security Advisor with a reputation for his strategic brilliance and Tuhina, an enigmatic and highly skilled operative from RAW, appeared on the screen, nodding in acknowledgment.

Raghav spoke first, his voice calm yet authoritative. "Congratulations to all including me. We have a complex and dangerous mission ahead of us and all of your expertise will be invaluable. I am sure we will be a wonderful team."

Tuhina added, her eyes sharp and focused. "The stakes are very high right now and we must work together seamlessly. The deeper we get into this, the more intricate it will become, therefore please stay connected."

The Prime Minister's voice resonated through the speakers. "Kavitha, this is a complex and dangerous situation. What are your recommendations?"

Kavitha's voice was steady yet urgent as she addressed the assembled team. "We need to gather more intelligence on the Arakan Army's connections and potential backers. These are the same nexus that toppled the Bangladeshi government. We need to strengthen our alliances with neighbouring countries; that will be very crucial. We also need to prepare to defend against the possibility of this conflict spilling over into our region."

The room fell silent as the weight of her words sank in. The Arakan Army's story was one side of power, conflict, and the struggle for autonomy and on another side, the illegal human trafficking of Rohingyas seeking political asylum, along with drugs and arms and illegal trafficking, along with the threat of fake currencies. Moreover, the threat of "Myth," the deadly narcotic to destabilize the backbone of any nation through widespread addiction in one side and in another side the fake currencies to jeopardize the economy of the nation with the defeated economy.

As the meeting progressed, tension filled the air. Shivansh, Riya, Aarav, and Meera exchanged glances, each of them grasping the enormity of the task ahead. They had faced challenges before, but this mission felt different, more daunting and the geographical bar was blurred.

Kavitha went on to say, "Illegal people trafficking networks, illegal substances, and phony currencies, including guns, are getting more brazen, taking advantage of the Rohingyas' desperate need for political sanctuary. This nexus became the most hazardous and dangerous since the spread of 'Myth' directly endangers our young, undermining the cornerstone of our civilization. We are dealing with numerous dangers that require a coordinated and deliberate response.

Raghav, the seasoned strategist, leaned forward. "We need to map out the key players and their motivations. Understanding their goals will allow us to anticipate their moves and effectively counter their techniques.

Tuhina, a counterintelligence expert, adding, "We should also investigate the deep state actors in Myanmar." They may be using these confrontations to keep power or distract from internal concerns."

Kavitha nodded, appreciating their insights. "Agreed. We must be thorough and unrelenting in our pursuit. Our connections with neighbouring countries need to be strengthened. This is more than simply our fight; it is a regional issue that necessitates a coordinated response."

The room was filled with newfound determination. Each team member understood the stakes were enormous, but they were prepared to face the obstacles head-on. The job was clear: find the truth, remove the chaos networks, and restore stability.

As the conference ended, Shivansh, Riya, Aarav, and Meera realized their quest had taken an unexpected turn. With these aims and plans in place, the team prepared to embark on a dangerous and unknown adventure.

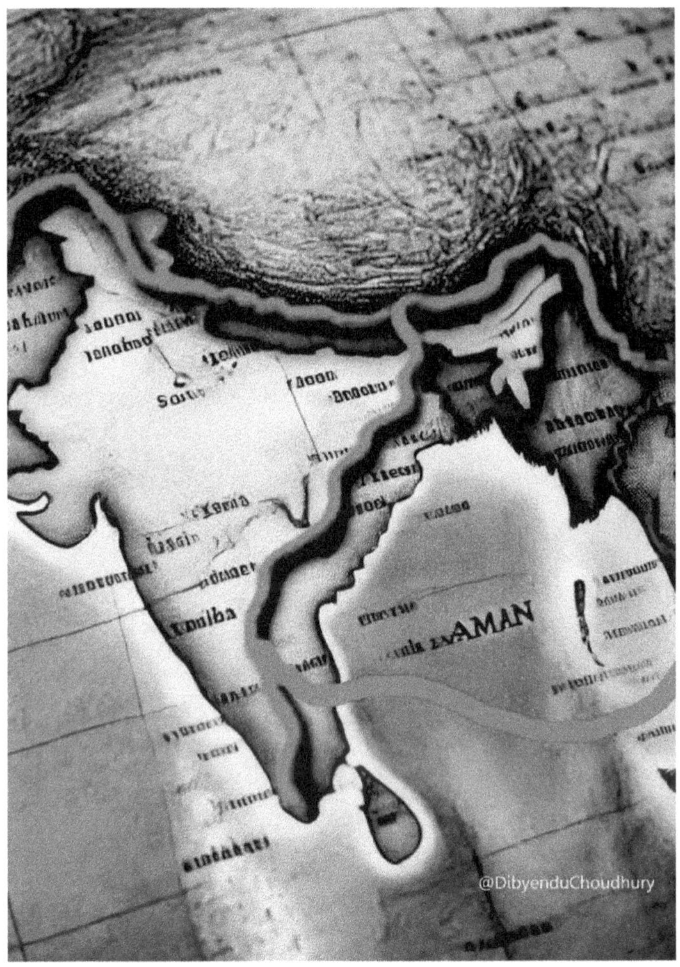
AMAN
@DibyenduChoudhury

TEKNAF BORDER-GATEWAY BETWEEN
BANGLADESH AND MYANMAR
Chapter-21

Chapter 21: Teknaf Border-Gateway Between Bangladesh and Myanmar

The Teknaf border had been a major crossing point between Bangladesh and Myanmar. It was situated on the Naf River in Bangladesh's southernmost district, Cox's Bazar. Maungdaw in Rakhine State was Myanmar's counterpart. Border Guard Bangladesh (BGB) personnel had been presented to provide security. Checkpoints and immigration stations had been utilized for legitimate crossings; however, they had all been removed owing to the current situation, and the Arakan Army (AA) had taken control of the border with the Naf River. This was the most opportune moment for both side illegal immigration to occur including the smuggling of goods and weapons.

Both Zakir and Rasheed left Dhaka three days ago, driving either Highway N1 or N104. Before heading to Cox's Bazar, pass through Comilla and Chittagong. Monsoon rains can produce flooding on the roads, which slows down travel time. There may be checkpoints along the way for security checks, particularly near the border. Auto-rickshaws go slower than cars or buses, especially on highways. Despite the impracticality of driving long distances, the auto-rickshaw could be used in clandestine or covert travel circumstances where maintaining a low profile is critical, such as escaping regular checkpoints or crossing rural backroads. They had travelled 450 kilometres in the last three days, stopping at various spots in their allies' homes.

The sun set below the horizon, leaving crimson and gold streaks in the sky above Bangladesh's southernmost point, the "Teknaf Border". The deep mangroves of the Sundarbans created spooky shadows on the gravel road, and Zakir slumped back in Rasheed's antiquated auto-rickshaw, his thoughts clouded with fear. Rasheed Khan, his rickshaw driver, appeared to be an experienced and all-time driver during his stay in Bangladesh: dependable, quiet, and tough. However, Zakir had no idea how this seemingly innocent man knew about the hidden nature of this trip and his rise to the agency's second-in-command in ISI.

The rickshaw bumped along the uneven trail, the silence between driver and passenger punctuated only by the occasional squawk of birds from the mangroves. Zakir finally broke the quiet.

"How far to the border, Khan?" he asked, his tone impatient.

Rasheed looked at him in the mirror, a little smile on his lips. "Another hour." There are no patrols along this road, thus it is safer. Patience will get us through, my friend. "Your friends are eagerly waiting for you on the other side."

Zakir nodded, his attention turning to the suitcase on his lap. Inside were carefully faked documents that revealed the meticulous efforts of ISI-backed activities. These would be critical to embedding their operatives in Myanmar as humanitarian workers, ostensibly assisting Rohingya refugees while secretly laying the framework for political upheaval in collaboration with the Arakhine Army (AA). The ultimate objective was to create a proxy state under ISI control and destabilize the area.

The rickshaw sputtered through the narrow, winding paths of the mangrove forest. The air was thick with the scent of wet earth and saltwater, and the sound of insects filled the night. Rasheed glanced at Zakir in the rearview mirror, his eyes calculating every move.

"We're almost there, brother. Are you ready for what's to come?" Rasheed asked, his voice calm yet authoritative.

"Yes, but I'm still not clear how you have all my information which I never disclose to anyone. What exactly is your role?" Zakir responded, his curiosity tinged with suspicion.

Rasheed's lips curled into a faint, almost imperceptible smile. "You'll know soon enough. Just follow the plan." Zakir found his tone becoming authoritative, sensing that Rasheed was not someone to be taken lightly.

As the rickshaw approached an inconspicuous house nestled in the mangroves, Rasheed pulled over and killed the engine. He turned to face Zakir, his expression turning serious.

"There's something you should know now because maybe, we will not be meeting again. Rasheed Khan was just a name. My real name is Ishtiaq Khan of ISI, and your reporting is directly with me in ISI," Rasheed revealed.

Zakir's eyes widened in shock. "Ishtiaq Khan? The Ishtiaq Khan? I... I've heard stories, but I never imagined..."

"Over the years, I've assumed many roles—a diplomat, a merchant, even a religious scholar—in different countries. Now, disguised as a humble auto driver in Bangladesh for the last five years with my wife, I'm overseeing one of the most delicate phases of our ongoing operation. I saw your work and dedication to the nation and you deserve the promotion. I will be retiring soon and in search of my successor." Ishtiaq Khan explained, his voice steady and unwavering.

Zakir sat back, trying to process the revelation. Ishtiaq Khan continued, "What you didn't know is that I'm not just your driver. I'm orchestrating the entire plan back in Pakistan and working in tandem with our team of gallant operatives too. We've already turned a senior member of Myanmar's AA. His loyalty was purchased through bribes and veiled threats. Your role is just a cog in the grand machine there."

Zakir nodded slowly, a newfound respect and fear for the man sitting in front of him. Ishtiaq Khan's eyes bore into him as he delivered his final instructions. "We never met, and we never talk. Our destination is that house. Go inside. My wife is inside; go take a shower and get some rest; I'll meet you both for dinner. Your guide will meet you here before or after midnight."

With that, Zakir obeyed silently, stepping out of the rickshaw and into the dimly lit house, his mind racing with the gravity of the situation.

Rasheed waited outdoors because of certain calls and reports and resources mobilization to his bosses at

Karachi; his thoughts drifted to the home he built in southern Bangladesh with his wife, Alina, whom he had renamed Afroz after their marriage. She was a Sri Lankan woman he met on one of his secret missions in Phuket, Thailand, several years ago. She had been working in the brothel where Rasheed frequently took refuge—not for pleasure, but to gather intelligence from the influx of high-profile guests. Regardless of her surroundings, Alina's fierce independence and caustic wit had charmed him. Over the years, their relationship had evolved into something Rasheed could not readily describe, but he was positive it was unlike anything he had ever experienced with any of the women he had been with. He knew Alina was the one he had been looking for all his life.

For a man steeped in shadows and lies, Alina was his only semblance of truth. She didn't know he was Ishtiaq Khan, the most wanted man in several nations' intelligence dossiers. To her, he was Rasheed—an elusive yet gentle partner who often disappeared for months without explanation.

Rasheed arrived later in the evening, as Alina was busy preparing the meal. She was aware of his presence because the visitors had entered their home. To her, this was just another of Rasheed's covert business travels, which occasionally took him back to the Bangladesh border after months away. He planned to live a peaceful life with his wife most of the time and retire here from his job, but she had to wait nearly a year to see him again. She never complained about his extended absences, nor was she concerned about his business. She was pleased with him, and she understood how hard Rasheed fought to get her out of Phuket to here.

As they sat down to dinner, Alina brought up a conversation she often revisited.

"Rasheed you'll be crossing 60 in couple of days, darling; you've done enough traveling. Enough of this constant movement. Why not settle here? With me." Her voice was hopeful, her eyes searching his.

For a moment, the hardened operative faltered. Alina's presence was a rare solace in his treacherous existence, but settling down was a fantasy he could never afford but chased for long. Still, tonight, under the weight of her gaze, he found himself confessing more than he intended in front of Zakir.

"You've changed me in ways I never thought possible, Afroz. You've given me something no mission, no operation, ever could—peace. But you have to understand, the life I live… it doesn't allow peace."

Alina reached across the table, her hand brushing his. "There's always a choice, Rasheed. You may not see it now, but there is always a way out."

"Yes, of course, there he is and I know this man will get me relieved sooner and become a successful torchbearer of our trade." He pointed to Zakir, who was savouring the delectable food that Tarique Khan, the head of the ISI's wife, prepared and explained how their love and devotion turned a superhuman into a regular guy.

As the night deepened, Zakir prepared to move. In the next room, Rasheed gave him final instructions, detailing the safe house waiting across the Myanmar border. Zakir departed, slipping into the night with his guide to cross the river; Rasheed stayed behind. He lit a cigarette, leaning against the doorframe, his thoughts clouded. It was a rare moment of vulnerability for the man who commanded the entire network spanning continents. On his direction, the entire nation and politics move along with the military intelligence.

Unbeknownst to him, Alina had been watching from the shadows, her brow furrowed. She had long suspected there was more to Rasheed than he let on, but she'd never pressed. Tonight, however, something felt different.

"What aren't you telling me, Rasheed?" She muttered under her breath, staring at his silhouetted figure against the moonlight.

As Rasheed returned inside, his phone buzzed. The name on the screen read Victor Lang.

"Lang," he answered, his tone icy.

"The shipment has reached Mandalay," Lang reported from Phuket. "Everything's in place. Zakir will finalize it when he reaches here."

"Good," Rasheed replied, his steely resolve returning. "But ensure this: no loose ends. If the plan is compromised, our presence here will not be traced. Burn the trail."

Lang hesitated before replying, "Understood."

As he ended the call, Rasheed cast a final glance at Alina, asleep in the bedroom. She was his tether to a world he could never truly inhabit—a life of love and simplicity.

Turning away, he muttered to himself, "The price of this life is too steep. It's time to rest and settle down forever."

The storm outside raged on, echoing the tempest within the man who had mastered deception yet longed for a sliver of truth.

Rasheed's double life teetered on the brink, each thread pulling closer to revelation. In the shadows, an unknown hand began unravelling the plans—because even the puppet master has enemies.

(To be continued….)